BLACK
HORNET

Also by JAMES SALLIS

BLACK
HORNET

JAMES SALLIS

Walker & Company
New York

First published in hardcover in the United States of America in 1994 by Carroll & Graff; this paperback edition published in 2003 by Walker Publishing Company, Inc.

Published simultaneously in Canada by Fitzhenry and Whiteside, Markham, Ontario L3R 4T8

For information about permission to reproduce selections from this book, write to Permissions, Walker & Company, 435 Hudson Street, New York 10014

Library of Congress Cataloging-in-Publication Data available upon request
ISBN 0-8027-7643-4 (paperback)

Visit Walker & Company's Web site at www.walkerbooks.com

Printed in Canada

2   4   6   8   10   9   7   5   3   1

To Joe Roppolo

BLACK
HORNET

1.

Back in basic, which turned out to be fully a fifth of my military career, there was a guy named Robert, a gangly young man from Detroit so black he seemed polished. We were all out on the range one afternoon. They'd hauled an old World War II tank out there, and we were supposed to step up to the line, assemble a molotov cocktail and lob it into the tank through the open hatch. My own toss, most of our tosses, missed pretty sadly. Then Robert toed up there. He stood a few seconds looking off at the tank and hefting the bottle, getting the weight of it. Then with an easy overhand, he dropped his cocktail squarely into the tank: just like a man walking through a door. His perpetual smile jacked up a half degree, no more. "Sort of thing come in handy back home," he said.

I remembered that, I think for the first time since it happened, when I read about the sniper.

His name was Terence Gully and he was twenty-three. He'd been in the Navy, but things hadn't gone well for him there. *Discrimination*, he told friends, ex-employers, would-be employers, people on the streetcar or at bus stops. So at eleven A.M. on a bright fall day Gully had lugged a .44-caliber Magnum rifle and a duffel bag full of ammunition up an old fire escape onto the roof of The King's Inn motel half a mile from City Hall, taken up position in a concrete cubicle there, and opened fire. Tourists and office workers on lunch break started going down before anyone knew what was happening. A Nebraska couple staying at the motel on their honeymoon, returning from breakfast. A couple of motel employees. A police officer who'd heard the first shots and rushed over from City Hall.

Hours later, bodycount mounting (bodycount being a term we were getting used to hearing in those years, *grâce à* LBJ and General Westmoreland), they brought in a Seaknight chopper from the naval air base at Belle Chase. As they flew in low over the roof preparing to open fire, the pilot and police heard Gully ranting below them: "Power to the people. . . . You'll never take me. . . . Africa! Africa!"

The pilot would later distinguish himself in Vietnam and return home, Purple Heart and Medal of Honor prominently displayed behind his desk, to a Ford dealership out in burgeoning Metairie, where mostly he sat in his glassed-in office and steadily poured Scotch into his coffee, himself a kind of exhibit now, as customers and their children ranged through the showroom beyond. One of the officers aloft with him that day, Robert Morones, would go on to become the city's youngest chief of police and eventually settle into the easy chair of perennial reelection to his seat in the state legislature.

The siege lasted over twelve hours and left in its wake fifteen dead, thirty or more injured, untold damage both from diversionary fires Gully had set and from returned police gunfire.

The siege also left in its wake a badly shaken city. There had always been a silent accommodation here, a gentlemen's agreement that blacks and whites would go on pursuing their parallel lives. But had the codes now changed? If one black man could carry his rage on his back onto a roof and from there hold hostage an entire city, if a group of black men (like those calling themselves Muslims) could recant their place in white man's society, if still other groups and individuals (Black Panthers, The Black Hand) openly advocated taking up arms against that society—what remnants obtained of *any* agreement? Or, finally, of society itself.

The man who cut your yard Monday noon and shuffled feet when he came for his pay might come after your possessions and station, your livelihood, your very life, Tuesday night.

Made you think of the city under Spanish rule circa 1794, when Governor Carondelet, perched on the edge of a chair the French Revolution was busily pulling out from under European complacencies, mindful how quickly this sort of thing might spread, encircled the city with walls and forts, not to turn away attackers, but to help contain (he thought) its own French citizens.

Floors and makeshift shelves at Terence Gully's Camp Street apartment were stacked with literature: pamphlets, flyers, tracts, hand-lettered posters. Over and over on the plasterboard walls Gully had scrawled peace signs, swastikas and slogans.

KILL THEM ALL!
BLACK IS RIGHT
HATE WHITE PEOPLE—BEASTS OF THE EARTH

The King's Inn shootings were one parochial incident all but lost among a hundred others in those years of mounting violence. The first Kennedy had already gone down. The Watts riots were just around the corner. Memphis was waiting for Martin Luther King, L.A. for Robert Kennedy, a lectern in the Audubon Ballroom, Harlem, for Malcolm X. A month or so before, fifteen black men and women in Sunday best had staged a sit-in at City Hall's basement cafeteria, where blacks weren't served, and were dragged away by police. Three civil rights workers would be killed up in Mississippi just months later.

Looking back now, 1968 seems pretty much the hub year, a fulcrum. During the summer Olympics in Mexico City two American athletes were suspended for giving a black-power salute. The Tet Offensive also started up that year—along with bloody racial riots on the unreported back lots of Vietnam.

Not that I was much up on current events at the time. I had my hands full just getting to know my new home: how to get around in New Orleans, how to slide through the days here, how to clip off enough to survive, how to get by. When you're young, history's not worth much. When you get older, whether you consider it baggage or burden, history's a large part of what you have. So a lot of this I learned, or relearned, later on.

Mostly what you lose with time, in memory, is the specificity of things, their exact sequence. It all runs together, becomes a watery soup. Portmanteau days, imploded years. Like a bad actor, memory always goes for effect, abjuring motivation, consistency, good sense.

So I couldn't have told you then, even with a knife at my throat (were you, for instance, some singular historical mugger intent upon relieving passersby of their lives' spare change), what year Vietnam got under way, when either Kennedy went down, what the Watts riots were *really* about.

Now I know.

But even then there were things you couldn't help knowing. You'd turn on the radio while shaving and between songs hear about men whose faces had been torn off. Drop by Alton's Barbershop, he'd snap the cloth around in front of you, and just for a minute, as both your eyes went to his big black-and-white set on a shelf above the cash register, the weight of the world would settle on you. The sky would fall. You'd feel your feet sink a little deeper into the ground.

And in New Orleans those days you couldn't get away from talk of the sniper. Wherever you went, whoever was talking, that was the subject. Like weather, it was everywhere.

Then someone stopped talking about it and started doing something.

Monday morning, mid-November. A young man walking along Poydras on his way between the parking space he rented by the month and his job at Whitney National fell as he started across Baronne and lay dying against the curb. He was wearing a suit, he was white, and he had been shot, once, through the chest. Police sealed off and searched the area to no avail.

Wednesday, again downtown, on Carondelet a block from Canal, another fell, an off-duty bus driver. Bystanders this time reported hearing shots spaced perhaps six seconds apart (investigators counted it out for them, to be sure), and said that the shots came from high up. A roof perhaps. Or one of the upper windows in this sole canyonlike stretch of the city. The bus driver had been struck first in the middle of his forehead, then squarely in the chest, through the sternum just above the ziphoid process.

Saturday the action moved uptown, to Claiborne, where a German tourist fell, dead before he hit the buckling sidewalk, as he exited a Chick'n Shack. Police found a single shell casing, already baked halfway into roofing tar, atop a boarded-up Holy Evangelical church nearby.

Police Chief Warren Handy told the public there was no cause for alarm. That the incidents did not appear to be related. And that, at any rate, the department ("I'm going on record here") anticipated speedy apprehension of whatever parties might prove responsible for this "horrendous outrage."

The Times-Picayune recycled Terence Gully stories, with new sidebars, and pointed out that all those shot were white. COPY-CAT KILLER, bold headlines announced the first day. GUERILLA LOOSE IN THE CITY? they asked the next. FIRST SHOTS OF A RACE WAR? the weekly newspaper *Streetcar* suggested.

Then on Wednesday, with a Loyola adjunct instructor dead in the street outside an apartment complex undergoing restoration on Jefferson, John LeClerque and Monica Reyna, hosts of WVUE-TV's six o'clock news (his toupee, her lisp and impossibly red lips in tow) blossomed to life onscreen before a headline in two-inch letters, stark black on white: ROOFTOP KILLER STRIKES AGAIN.

2.

" 'Lo, Lew."

I returned his cool regard. We were all into cool those days: cool regards, cool threads and music, cool affairs. Hand-slapping, tribal handshakes and high fives hadn't yet quite caught on.

"You got it," I told Sloe Eddie. "Sometimes low, other times high."

One night, ten years ago at least, Eddie had gone sailing on sloe gin fizzes and not hove back into port for almost a week; he'd earned the nickname for life.

"You get high enough you'n see *all* the shit."

"So they tell me. Like we don't see enough of it down here."

"Got *that* right."

"You coming?"

"Going. Two young ladies and a new bottle of Cutty waitin' for me. Your man's hot tonight, though."

I went on inside, sat at the end of the bar, and ordered a Jax.

The club, like most of them, smelled of mildew, urine, beer, and edgy, cheap alcohol. Twenty or thirty years ago someone had scraped together enough money to buy the place, nailing down his piece of American dream, turning the gleam in his eye momentarily real. He'd hired a crew of workmen. They'd begun fixing it up: excavated studs preparatory to tacking up prefab panels, laid new Formica along part of the bar, soldered temporary patches on bathroom plumbing. But then the money ran out, a lot quicker than Someone had anticipated, and his crew jumped ship.

Most of the club's patrons had jumped ship too, from the look of it. A scatter of couples at the tables, a teenage hooker dropping shots of Smirnoff's like clear stones into beer.

The TV over the bar was on, some show about a paraplegic chief of police, the premise of which seemed to be that a cripple, a woman and a young black man, together, made up a single effective human being. The young black guy pushed the chief's wheelchair around, and the show was set in San Francisco. I kept on waiting for YBM to push the damned thing to the top of one of those famous hills and let go. There'd be this gorgeous minute or so of "Blue Danube" or "Waltzing Matilda" as the wheelchair plunged ever faster down hill after hill into traffic, doom, the bay.

Against the back wall, in the light of a portable spot, Buster was giving it everything he had. He always did. There'd been nights the bartender and I were the only ones around, and even then I couldn't tell a difference.

Light spurred off the sunburst finish of his Guild as he leaned back in the chair and threw his head up. The steel tube on his finger glinted, too, as it slid along the strings. Both feet struck the floor, levered up on their heels, struck again.

Sun goin' down, dark night gon' catch me here.
Said sun goin' down, mmmmm night gon' catch me here.
Don't have no woman, love and feel my care.
Mmmm, mmmm, mmmm, mmmm.

Those last mmmm's on the two-bar turnaround: E, E-7th, A-7th, B-7th.

I'd learned a lot about the blues from Buster Robinson.

I'd learned a lot from Buster, period.

He'd cut a couple dozen sides for Bluebird and Vocalion in the early forties when they were called race records and sold at grocery stores for a nickel apiece, and they'd done all right. But then Buster got in a fight over a woman at a rent party he was playing, the other guy got dead, and Buster went up for a stretch at Parchman. And by the time he got out, musical tastes (he told me) had just plumb left him behind.

For the past thirty-six years Buster had worked as a barbeque cook up in Fort Worth, at a take-out joint off Rosedale near the hospitals there, an old Spur station with pumps still standing out front. Then the folk revival came along. Some enterprising college kid from back East decided he might not be dead after all, as everybody assumed, and somehow had managed to track him down. Buster didn't even have a guitar, hadn't played one in over twenty years. So the kid and his friends chipped in and bought him one. Then one Saturday they all came over to Buster's place, put a bottle of Grandad and a tape recorder on the kitchen table, and let the recorder run for the next hour while Buster played, sang, got mildly drunk ("cause I's a *Christian* man now, you see") and talked about old times.

The kids pressed it just the way they recorded it and it sold like Coke.

But orders kept coming in, and Kid and Friends weren't prepared, financially or by temperament, to tack into this new wind. They wound up selling all rights to BlueStrain. Strain (as everybody called it) had had remarkable success issuing live-recorded jazz on a label previously known for classical recordings. The recovering beats and MBA's who ran BlueStrain were convinced that Buster Robinson was a shoo-in as the next Mississippi John Hurt.

It took them about two months to decide that what money they were going to make off B.R., they'd *already* made. The new pressing didn't sell. Everyone who wanted it had it. And no one came to the live concerts in Boston, Philly, Gary, Des Moines, Cleveland, Memphis.

So BlueStrain cut Buster loose.

> *Sometime I live in de city,*
> *Sometimes I live in town.*
> *Sometime I takes a great notion*
> *To jump into de river an' drown.*

"In-to-the" a perfect suspended triplet.

The teenage hooker peered out from the crow's nest of her solitude, saw land heaving up nowhere in sight, and ordered another boilermaker. *Outer Limits* with its monster-of-the-week, animal, vegetable, mineral, appeared onscreen.

How I met Buster is a story in itself, I guess.

I'd been working collections freelance at a straight percentage. I was big enough and looked mean enough to get most people's attention, which was all it really took. And after a while I started getting something else: a reputation. I saddled it, rode it, never put it up wet. But a reputation cuts both ways. Recently I'd had to step on a couple of guys feeling their balls and not about to be told what to do by no jive-ass nigger. One of them got hurt kind of bad. I went to see him on a ward at Mercy afterward but he didn't have much to say to me. Fuck you, as I recall, being pretty much it.

Boudleaux & Associates was turning a lot of work my way those days. B&A operated out of a sweltering, unpainted cinderblock office on South Broad across from McDonald's and the Courthouse and consisted of a P.I named Frankie DeNoux who lived off Jim's fried chicken. All the years I knew him, I never saw him eat anything else. Always a cardboard tray of breasts and thighs on the desk, grease spreading out from its base onto various legal documents, invoices, paperback spy novels, check ledgers; always a cooler of Jax to wash it down. Undrunk coffee forever burning to sludge on the hotplate alongside.

Frankie weighed a hundred pounds in eight-pound shoes. Despite his diet and the fact that he never saw sunlight and hadn't so much as walked around the block in forty years, he was fit and trim and probably could have picked up the office and carried it down the street on his shoulder. He was already three times my age and, I was sure, would outlive me. "Don't matter what jew eat, what jew do or don't do," he said frequently. " 'S all genetics." He pronounced it *gene-etics.*

"Want some chicken?" he asked one day when I dropped by to see if he had anything for me. Collections, papers that needed serving, whatever. Jobs were getting scarce. People had suddenly stopped acting like they had money they didn't have, and my own strictly-cash economics showed the wear.

Frankie picked up the greasy carton and held it out.

I shook my head. "No, sir. But thank you."

He redocked it.

You didn't often find a white man offering to eat after a black one those days, even in New Orleans.

It made me remember my father and me back in Arkansas ordering breakfast through a window to the kitchen of Nick's (where the cooks were all black, the customers all white) and eating it on the steps of the railroad roundhouse by the levee at five A.M. It was godawful cold, forty degrees maybe, with wind shouldering in off the river. My father's breath, when he spoke to me of the life I could expect there, plumed out and mixed with the steam rising off grits and eggs.

"You sure?" Frankie said, *r* drawn out, New Orleans-style, to *wuh*.

"Yes, sir." My own *r* carefully sounded.

"Don't know what you're missing."

He fingered a drumstick out of the tray. Bit into it, rotated, bit again. Put the bone with its cap of browned gristle back.

"Best dam' food 'n the world."

"You've got something for me, Mr. Frankie?"

"Sure I do." Shu-wuh. "I ever *not* had something for you?"

"So: what? I have to guess? That it?"

He grinned. "Two hundred a week."

"Okay. You got my attention."

"First week guaranteed, possible re-up for two more. Could be a lot longer."

"Mm-*hm*."

"Man called, tells me he needs a bodyguard. Says he's heard good things about B&A, the service we provide, wonders if I might know someone could do the job."

"And it just happens you did."

"Yep."

"Me."

"You." He picked a wing out of the carton, pulled off the skin and ate that, then nibbled away till bone was again glistening.

"I wouldn't even know how to start."

"What's to know? You walk him aroun'. Swing your dick, give anyone the eye gets too close, pick up your money."

I could probably do that.

"You know an easier way to bank a few hundred?"

I didn't know any other way at all.

That first client was a local city councilman being groomed for national elections. Though he sat high on public-opinion polls, grievous differences between him and his wife's family persisted. For one thing, that was where his money came from, and her old Creole family grieved at seeing Greatgranddaddy's wad used to nurture unseemly liberal causes. Neither were they sympathetic to the mistress who'd been his student in Poly Sci at Loyola or the one who lived over Gladfellows Lounge with its neon martini glass (where she worked) on St. Charles.

Threats had been voiced, more serious ones implied.

Councilman Fontenot, as it turned out, made one of those clear choices he was always talking about in campaign speeches and took the Hollywood high road: true love over career. Two weeks after I joined the troupe he jumped ship and moved in with his coed.

Fontenot had a passion for old black music and young white women. Two or three nights a week, myself in tow and doing my best to look suitably dangerous, he'd tour the Negro clubs along Dryades and Louisiana. He especially liked listening to Buster.

So did I, and long after the councilman tucked himself away in his coed's drawers, I went on showing up wherever Buster was playing. There wasn't any work for a while, and since I was around every night, Buster and I started getting friendly. I'd sit sipping beers during his sets, then afterward we'd crack a bottle there at the club or back at Buster's. He'd play and sing this incredible stuff I never even knew existed. Robert Johnson, Charlie Patton, Willie McTell, Sonny Boy Williamson.

Eventually there was no reprieve from it, I had to get back to work. Off and on I'd still drop by clubs where Buster was playing, as I did that autumn night, but it was never the same. When's it *ever* the same once you've left?

The night I told Buster I wouldn't be around anymore, we got so drunk that toward morning he fell out of his chair and smashed the big Gibson twelve-string he'd just bought. I woke up hours later on the levee, with my legs in the water. I remember raising my head and looking at them just kind of bobbing about down there in the wake from ferries and tugs, bobbing along with the candy wrappers, paper cups and other flotsam that had collected around them.

3.

"Lewis. Been a while." He was wiping his head and neck with a dish towel as he nodded. A quick, shallow nod you could miss if you weren't ready for it. "Been a *long* while." The barkeep slipped a tumbler of jug wine, three ice cubes, onto the bar in front of him. Buster nodded at him, too. "I'm in danger or what, get you out this time a night?"

"We may all be."

"Not less you done turned white, Lewis. Have to tell you, I always thought you might have that in you." He laughed.

"Yeah, well. It's hard enough being a black man in this town now, B.R. Way things are going, it could soon get a lot harder."

He looked at me a moment. "See your point. Crazy gon' always make room for more of the same." He slapped the towel across a shoulder. "But *damn* it's good to see you, boy."

"You too."

"And looking *good*. That jacket silk?"

"Better be, what I gave for it."

"Stayin' busy, I hope."

"Rent gets paid. Most of the time, anyway."

"And Miss Verne?"

"She's fine."

"She *is* for sho'. That's a stone fact." He sipped wine. "Whoo-*ee*. Raccoon must of pissed in the cask that year. Let's go find us a place."

13

I followed him to one of the booths at the back. Maybe half the upholstery and stuffing was still hanging on. Some kind of plastic film had been put up in the window there, each pane a different color, gold, bottle green, purple, a stained-glass effect. Now the film had baked dry and started chipping away at the edges.

"So who you think this is? Got to be a brother."

I shrugged. "Not my business."

"Not *yet*, anyway. Like you say." He sipped wine again, drew his lips tight against his teeth.

A man about my age wearing a baseball cap, jeans and dashiki came in off the street and stood by the door peering into the darkness. Moments later, he stood by our booth.

"You Robinson?"

Again that quick, shallow nod.

"Ellie ain't goan be here tonight like she prob'ly tole you. Fact is, she ain't goan ever see you no more a-tall."

Buster drank off an inch of wine. Set the glass back on the table, in the same ring it had left. Smiled.

"Woman'll do what she's called to, boy. Cain't you or no one else on God's earth keep her from it."

The young man held up a knife. It had started out as a butcher knife. The handle had been replaced with tape and both sides worked down to a fine edge. It looked cold, dark, deadly.

"Then I just might haf to fix things so you won't haf a int'rest no longer. Fix *yo'* things. You hear me, ol' man?"

I eased around the curve of the table and stood, hands out in front of me, fingers spread.

"Hey. Be cool, brother. You have a name?"

His eyes swung momentarily to me, then back to B.R.

"He knows."

"But I don't."

He thought about that. "Cornell."

"Okay, Cornell. Just be cool. Whatever the problem is, we can talk about it. You look like a smart man to me, someone might know his way around. Just put the knife away, okay? Let's keep it simple."

"You stay out of it, man."

"Can't do that," I told him.

The edge in my voice brought his eyes back to me.

Moments ticked by. Threw themselves over that edge.

"Who the fuck *are* you? Whatchu doin' here?"

"Passing time with an old friend. Not looking for trouble. Neither is he. My name's Lew Griffin."

"Griffin ... I heard once about a Lew Griffin. Came round to my grandparents to collect on some furniture they took on payments—"

"My job, Cornell."

"—and wound up giving them money enough for two months. You wouldn't be *that* Lew Griffin?"

"They seemed like good people." Though damn if I remembered them.

"Yeah. Raised me and three sisters, no help from anyone, never a complaint. And they was already in their sixties."

He looked back at me.

"They gone now."

"I'm sorry."

"Things just ain't ever as easy as they seem, are they?"

"Not usually."

"Lot better if they were."

"Maybe someday they will be."

Cornell's eyes went back and forth.

"That ol' man goan leave my woman alone?"

"I'm sure he will, now he knows how you feel."

"Need to hear *him* say it."

B.R. shrugged.

Further moments plunged off the edge.

"Well," Cornell said. "Guess I do owe you one, Lew Griffin, rememberin' my grandparents and all. Don't owe *that* nigger nothing, though. 'Cept pure hurt, he ever think 'bout messin' with my Ellie again."

Cornell turned away as though to leave. If it was only subterfuge from the first, or if suddenly he gave in to impulse, buckled under to the tug and tumble of his emotions, I'll never know. But he wheeled back around. His knife slashed through the space where moments ago my throat had been.

I had watched his center of gravity start to shift, muscles begin bunching, and was already rolling away clockwise when he turned.

Now I rode my own momentum full circle. Dropped to a squat as I went on around, drove clasped hands against his right knee.

I felt something in there snap as he went down hard. Only ligaments, I hoped.

I reached up and took the knife. When I stood, Buster grinned at me.

"What's a lonely ol' man like me to do? She's so sweet, Lew."

"Sweet."

"Pure as sugar cane." He finished off his tumbler of wine and got up. "Back on the horse. Anything you specially want to hear, Lew?"

" 'Black Snake Moan' might be appropriate."

Buster rejoined his guitar. Somehow he never looked quite right without it; you had a sense of missing body parts. Dampening the A string with the heel of his hand while hammering at it with his thumb, he started a vamp on the top strings, all pull-offs and bends.

Mmmmmm, mama what's the matter now.

Someone beside me said: "Buy you a drink?"

She wore a denim skirt, wool sweater, Levi jacket. Her hair was shorter than in her picture. Light brown, with a lot of red.

"Figure you could probably use one."

"Okay."

We went over and sat at the bar. The barkeep slid a bottled Lowenbrau, glass inverted over it, in front of me. I thanked both of them.

"You're welcome," she said.

So we sat there, me with my beer, her with her Scotch on the rocks, Buster singing about going back to Florida where you gotta plow or you gotta hoe. "Someone coming to take care of the boy?" I asked the barkeep. He shrugged. But eventually a Charity ambulance pulled up out front and two fat white guys came in to fetch him.

The woman sat watching them. When they were gone she held up two fingers and the barkeep brought another round. She picked hers up, sniffed at it, swirled it around the squat glass and put it down without drinking.

"Ever hear of O'Carolan?"

I shook my head.

"He was a minstrel, I guess. A wandering musician. Wrote a lot of music for Irish harp. Supposedly on his deathbed he asked for a glass of whiskey, saying 'It'd be a terrible thing if two such good friends were to part without a final kiss.' "

She turned toward me on her stool and held out a hand.

"You're Lew Griffin. I—"

"Yes, m'am. I know who you are."

Her face appeared three days a week atop a *Times-Picayune* column. Mostly light humor about how difficult life was for uptown white women. You know: finding the right caterer, when to wear white shoes, getting the kids off to camp. But every so often she got her teeth into something real. And when she did, the city's blood, the bottomless despair and pain running in it, squeezed out around her words.

"I spend a lot of time sitting in bars all over the city drinking too much cheap Scotch and bourbon, or in restaurants drinking coffee I don't want, talking to people some, but mostly listening to them. Past months, your name's come up in some oddly disparate places."

Oddly disparate. People who grow up on State Street or Versailles and go to Sophie Newcomb talk like that.

"First I heard about this guy who used to come around collecting for a shyster furniture-and-appliance outfit over on Magazine. He'd wind up telling people how to get out from under—even give them money for payments sometimes. A young Negro, they said. Big, wiry. Almost always wore a black suit. Shirt and tie.

"Then, in a different neighborhood, I'd hear how this same man walked into a French Quarter bar looking for someone who'd jumped bail and walked back out with his man, leaving behind, on the floor, a couple of hard customers with broken arms and cracked ribs."

She picked up her drink and took a long draw off it. Lowered her eyelids in respect as the taste took hold.

"I had to start wondering if there wasn't a story here."

"No, m'am, I don't think so."

"I'm painfully aware that I'm at least twice your age, you

know. But please don't call me m'am. That makes me feel even older. Esmé. Or just Ez—that's what most people call me.''

I nodded. She looked his way and the bartender, who was keeping his eye on her, hustled over with another round.

Buster retuned to standard and started a slow shuffle in E, improvising lyrics about Lewis Black and his Uptown Lady. I shot him a hard stare. He grinned.

So did Esmé. "Listen," she said, "they're playing our song.''

"You want a story?"

"At least three times a week.''

"Then there it is." I nodded toward Buster and started telling her about him. All those old records, how you'd trip over his name in books on blues and jazz history, the time he put in at Parchman, how he'd spent half his life cooking barbeque in an old gas station up in Fort Worth.

We went through that round and another as I talked. Esmé asked if I'd excuse her a minute. She was on the phone maybe a quarter hour, then came back.

"Calling in my column. Work's done. So now I can relax and have fun. No more grown-up for a while.''

The next morning on my way home from the police station, numb with fatigue, shaky with the adrenaline still sputtering in my veins, I'd read her piece about Buster, titled simply "A Life.'' And in days to come I'd read it over and over again, vainly seeking some final clue, some personal message or explanation, some reason that wasn't there.

"And what might that fun consist of?" I asked.

"Well, I *am* open to suggestion. But another drink and then dinner with a handsome young man is one definite possibility.''

"Will I do instead?"

"Oh, I suspect you'll do very nicely, Lewis.''

Another drink turned into several, the club slowly filled with bodies, Buster careened from Carter Family to Bo Chatmon to Chicago blues.

Finally we walked out into a warm, bright night. Across the street, leaves of banana trees moved slowly in the breeze, throwing terrible huge shadows across walls and sidewalk. Behind us Buster complained that his woman had waited till it was nine below zero and put him down for another man.

"Which way?"

"Depends. What are you in the mood for?"

"Creole? French?"

"Animal, vegetable or mineral."

"Mexican."

"Greek."

"Fried cardboard."

"That even sounds good. I'm starved."

"Me too."

"*Food*. For the love of God, Montressor." Hand held before her, fingers clawing feebly for purchase, eyes rolling back.

I had just reached out for that hand—our fingers, I think, barely grazed—when she fell. I looked down at the puncture in her forehead, just beneath the hairline, thick blood rimming over.

I remembered hearing the sound then and, though I knew there would be nothing to see, looked up.

For just a moment I thought I saw something move on one of the rooftops, a shadow crossing the moon. But of course I could not have.

4.

I counted twelve police cars pulled up at various angles on the street by the time I was put inside one (hand lightly on my head as I was urged into the backseat) and taken downtown. Most of them had flashers going. It looked like one of those carnivals that unfolds out of two trucks and takes over a whole parking lot.

At the station the cuffs were removed, I was given coffee, and for several hours, riders changing from time to time but always the same tired old pony, we played What-was-the-exact-nature-of-your-relationship-to-the-deceased.

It was all pretty much stage whispers and much ado. They knew I wasn't involved in the shooting. But black man/white woman was a formula they just couldn't leave alone. That people were getting shot like paper targets out there in the streets was nothing compared to *this* danger. Eternal vigilance.

"Come on, Griffin. Own up to it. You were lovers. Had to be. We know that."

He lit a cigarette, pushed the pack an inch or two across the table toward me.

"We look into it, we're gonna find out maybe she paid rent, bought your clothes, kept you in booze. Save us all some time here, boy."

"What was it, she started asking for something back? A little responsibility, maybe?" This from a wiry guy leaning against the wall behind the smoker.

21

"We got ten, twelve reporters lined up out there waiting to talk to someone, boy. Trying their damnedest to dig up a photo of you, *any* photo, they can run with their stories. Mayor's already called the chief—his and Ms. Dupuy's family go way back—and the chief's called me. Chief's waiting up for me to get back to him."

"We got to lay this off on someone soon, and I might as well tell you, we don't much care who it is."

"Shit deep enough you gonna need a *big* boat, anyway you come at it."

The wiry guy pushed himself away from the wall. His shoes were thirteens at least. On him, they looked like clown shoes.

"Someone said she'd have you make ape noises toward the end of things. Said that was the only way she could get off. That right?"

Dead silence. Smoke rolled about the room, thick as fog.

"You wanta just wait outside, Solly?"

"I—"

"*Now?*"

He waited till the other was gone.

"Lewis, we're trying to do you a favor, man. Just tell us the truth. What you could be looking at, it's prob'ly ten to twenty, even with good behavior. Your behavior likely to be good?"

I told him I doubted it.

"Somehow I do too."

I didn't have a record, that came later; but as I said, my name was on the streets some, even then.

I kept on trying to give them what they expected. Never met an eye, said yessir till my voice went hoarse, kept my head down. Along about daylight I decided what the hell, this dead horse had been beaten enough for one day.

"Sir," I said. "Don't you think I should have an attorney present?"

I figured they'd either shoot me or club me over the head and throw me out back with the rest of the trash. And at that point either one sounded preferable to more of the same.

"Why of course I do. I even believe you people, you're brought up right, you're good as anybody else. But the fact of the thing is, I can hold you for as long as I need to and ain't nobody going to say anything."

"On what charge?"

"Lewis, Lewis." He shook his head. "Where you been, boy? I don't need any charges."

"Maybe that will change."

"Maybe. But it ain't yet. Meanwhile you're a nigger. You been consortin' with a white woman got herself killed last night. You got no steady employment, got a hist'ry of violence, discharged from the service after beating in a few heads. You'll be lucky you even make it far as a cell."

He made a great show of packing his Winston down, snapping it repeatedly against a heavy Zippo lighter with some kind of military emblem on it. He put the cigarette in his mouth, thumbed the lighter's wheel and held it there.

"You boys come down here with a hard-on from—what? Arkansas? Mississippi?—and the city turns you inside out. You got some bad friends out there. Every day goes by, you sink a little further into the scum that coats this city a foot deep."

He brought lighter to cigarette, a small ceremony.

There was a rap at the door. The wiry guy stuck his head in.

"See you a minute, Sarge."

He went over and they stood there talking.

First I could make out only occasional words. Then, as their voices rose, more.

"... come down ..."

"... bust ... desk jockey ... wipe his nose ..."

"... collar comes off, like it or not ..."

"Fuck that."

"More like fuck you, Sarge."

"Yeah, like always."

He came back.

"You're free to go, Griffin."

"Just like that?"

He nodded. I started to say something else, ask what the hell, but he stopped me. "Get on out of here."

The city was just coming alive outside. Soft gray bellies of clouds hung overhead, as though draped, tentlike, on the top of the buildings. Sunlight snuffled and pawed behind them.

And Frankie DeNoux sat on the steps.

I almost didn't recognize him, since he wasn't wearing his office.

"Sweet freedom," he said.

"Believe it. But what are you doing here? Boudleaux finally throw you out? Whoever Boudleaux is." Far as I knew, no one had ever seen him. "You on the streets now?"

"Ain't that the way it always is. Do a favor for a guy, he won' even talk to you after."

"What favor's that, Mr. Frankie?"

"Sweet freedom," he said again.

I just stared at him.

"Got me a man up there. He keeps me posted what's going down, I slip him a fifty ever' week or so. Las' night he calls to let me know this woman's been shot and the police've brought in this guy he knows does some work for me. But the guy ain't been charged with nothin', he says, ain't even on the books.

"Well. This, I know, is definitely not good. Bad things happen in police stations to people who are not there. I know this from working with the criminal element, and with the police element, for forty years. After forty years, I also know a few people. Favors get owed along the way."

Closing the rest of his fingers, he held thumb and pinky finger out: a stand-up comedian's phone.

"I made some calls."

"You made some calls."

"Well, really it was just one. The other guy wouldn't talk to me. But . . ." He waved a hand: here's the free world anyway.

"I didn't know you had friends, period, Mr. Frankie. Much less friends in high places."

"High, low, scattered in between. Lots of those won't talk to me anymore either. What the hell. 'S all information, Lewis. You got information, you get things. You got things, you get information."

I was with him so far. But there was one point I wasn't clear on:
"Why?"

"Why, you got work to do for me, don't you. Now how you gonna do that locked up in there? Or with your mouth all busted up—you tell me that."

"Seems obvious, now that I think about it."

"Don't it, though."

"I owe you, Mr. Frankie."

"You don't owe me shit, Lewis. And don't Mr. Frankie me. Back up there, that was mostly smoke. What they call a dog and pony show. But you feel like saying thank you, there's a Jim's right round the corner. You could come have some chicken, sit down with me. Forty years I been eating alone.''

I said I'd be pleased to, and we walked on.

"Man might be dropping by to see you sometime later on. He does, you talk to him for me.''

"Yes, sir.''

"Don't sir me either.'' I held the door open for him. There were a couple of people in line ahead of us. A city bus driver. A rheumy-eyed white man in bellbottom jeans, grimy sweater and longshoreman's cap. "You know that story 'bout the tar baby?'' Frankie said.

I nodded.

"Well, that's 'bout how black my mother was, Lewis. Black as tar. I ain't been white a day in my life and ever'body's always thought I was. Ain't that somethin'?''

We stepped up to the counter.

"You want white meat or dark?'' he said, and laughed.

5.

Home those days was a slave quarters behind a house at Baronne and Washington that once had been grand and now looked like Roger Corman's idea of a Tennessee Williams set. Ironwork at gate and balcony had long ago gone green; each story, floor, room, door and window frame sat at its own peculiar angle; vegetation grew from cracks in cement walls and from the rotten mortar between bricks. Few of the porch's floor planks were intact, many were missing entirely. One vast corner column had burst open. Tendrils of onion plants snaked out from within it.

The slave quarters, however, were in fine repair. In the final decades of its grandness the house had been owned and occupied by the alcoholic, literarily inclined last son of an old New Orleans family. Day after day he sat drinking single-malt Scotch and punching forefingers at his father's Smith Corona while the house crumbled without and his liver dissolved within. And while his mother finally relocated to the slave quarters out back, as though moving to another state, and went on about her life.

Basically, I had two rooms, one stacked atop the other. Downstairs was a brief entryway with a niche for a couple of chairs to the left and closet-size bathroom to the right, then the kitchen and wooden stairs up to the living-bed-dining-room. There'd been a garden outside when I moved in, but rats had eaten everything down to stubble and memory.

The place was cheap because no one else wanted to live there—

either in the neighborhood, or behind that house. Most of those who *had* moved in over the years never made the second month's rent.

But I loved it. No one would ever find me here. It was like living in a secret fortress or on an island, cut off from the mainland by the house and high stone wall. And it was private, or had been until the house's porch fell in and its baker's dozen of renters all started coming and going by the back door, two yards from my front (and only) one.

Returning from my evening as a guest of the city, I walked through a gap in the wall and along the remains of a cement path that once ran the house's length.

Someone stood knocking at the door of the slave quarters.

As I said, no one could find me here. No one's *supposed* to find me here.

So what did no one want?

Instinctively slumping to make myself look smaller, I shuffled that way, talking as I went.

"See I'm not the *only* one looking for Mr. Lewis. No answer, huh? Man ain't *never* home! This my third trip all the way up here. He owe you money too?"

The man took his fist away from the door and put it in the pocket of his blazer. It had made the trip before; the cloth there was badly misshapen and the coat hung low on that side. Tan slacks, a wrinkled white cotton shirt and loose brown knit tie that all somehow had the feel of a uniform about them, as though he might wear these same clothes day after day.

"Don't suppose you'd have any idea where he is? Couple things I need to ask him about."

"Man, I don't even know what he *looks* like, you know? Boss just says: We got complaints on Blah-Blah, go find him. So I do. *Usually* do, anyway."

"Possible I might be able to help you there, seeing as I have a pretty good description. Big man, usually wears a black gabardine suit, tie. Course, that could be most anyone." He grinned. "You, for instance."

"Well. No way you're the Man, black as *you* are."

He took the hand back out of his pocket and extended it. "You have to be Griffin."

I shook it. "I do indeed. However hard I try not to be sometimes."

"And you know, I bet sometimes you almost make it."

"Almost."

"Don't we all, brother. And we just keep right on trying." When we let go, his hand crept back to the pocket. I don't think he even noticed anymore. "I'm Arthur Straughter, but everybody calls me Hosie. You got a few minutes?"

I shrugged, then nodded.

"Something I'd like to talk to you about. But not here. You ever take a drink this early in the morning?"

"It's been known to happen. Especially when I've still not been to bed. But I'd have to ask, first, what your business is with me."

"Fair enough. Miss Dupuy . . . Esmé and I . . ."

He looked off at the wall. No cues written on it. His face every bit as unreadable.

"She meant a lot to me, Griffin. We were together almost six years. And I can't begin to tell you what I'm feeling now. I'm not even sure myself. But you were with her at the end, you were the last person saw her alive. I thought maybe we could talk about that, what Ez did, what she said. I don't know why I think that might help. But it might. What *else* do I have?"

"A few last words," I said.

"Right. Like Goethe's *More Light!*, Thoreau's *Moose! Indians!* Or the grammarian: *I am preparing to, or I am about to, die. Either may be used.* I did an article on last words once. Now the most important thing in my life's just happened, and I know I'll never write about it.

"But if you can spare me half an hour or so, Griffin, I'd appreciate it. And I'll be in your debt."

We walked toward Claiborne, to a place called the Spasm Jazzbar flanked by a storefront Western Union and Hit and Run Liquors, in one of those easy silences that can settle in unexpectedly. Two feet past the open door, the bar itself was as dark and fraught with memory as Straughter's thoughts must have been. Whatever burdens came in here never left; they remained, became a part of the place, piled up atop previous layers.

A couple of walkers sat together at the bar. Both looked over their shoulders as we entered. I knew one of them, a friend of Verne's they called Little Sister on the street, a white girl who always worked the colored parts of town. Little Sister said something to her companion and they both turned back to their daiquiris.

Straughter and I stopped off at the bar for double bourbons on our way to a table in the back corner. Chairs were still inverted on the table. Not that the place ever closed, but they shoved things around and ran a mop through from time to time. Then the invisible layers, the real refuse, would part to let the mop pass and close like a sluggish sea behind it.

"I'm sorry. I really don't know what else to say. I've never had anyone I loved—" I became aware of my pause elongating "—die."

But I went on to tell him about B.R., about the fight, how Esmé and I had met in the wake of it all. The way she crossed her legs and slumped down in the chair and held her glass up to whatever light there was, constantly checking levels, color, how the world looked through that amber lens—as though placing it between herself and the light of some pending eclipse.

He must know all this, I said.

Yes, of course. But the particulars are what matter.

"We decided to go get some food. Dunbar's, maybe. Or Henry's Soul Kitchen. That time of night, a mixed party, choices were limited."

She didn't talk a lot about you, I told him.

When in fact she'd said nothing at all.

"Funny, but even after she called in her story and said now she could relax, she still listened more than she talked. Watching people, listening to them, the way they moved, how they leaned in and out of conversations. Always somehow apart. I guess she never got far away from that. All these stories, all these lives, went on spinning around her.

"So she didn't say much. Asked me a lot of questions about *my* life. But about her own, from what little she *did* say, I definitely had a sense of strength at the center, at the core."

"Me."

"You."

Straughter went up to the bar and brought back new drinks.

"Thanks," he said. "I appreciate your telling me that. And I want you to know that my appreciation is in no way diminished by your story's being an utter lie."

I started to protest, but he cut me off.

"Ez would *never* have spoken to anyone about me. Not once in all these years did she talk to anyone else about our life together. She just plain would not do it."

I spread my hands on the table between us. What could I say?

"But the rest, I'm grateful to you for that. Sometimes the smallest souvenirs turn out to be the best ones, with time."

"I don't really see how I could have helped."

"But you did. Want one more?"

"Sure, but it's my turn. Beer okay?"

I put the bottle in front of him and asked how he found me.

"You don't know who I am, do you?"

Later, I'd learn about Hosie Straughter. How he came down from Oxford, Mississippi, at age seventeen, self-taught and dressed in hand-me-downs, and ten years later won a Pulitzer. How he got fired from *The Times-Picayune* for writing a series on race relations in the city (only a part of the first installment ever saw print) and, on a wing and a prayer and small donations from middle-class black families, began publishing his own weekly, *The Griot*. Over the years he had become a voice not only for blacks, but for *all* the city's eternal outsiders, all its dispossessed. A voice that was listened to.

"No matter," he said. "I'm a journalist: you know that. So I have my own ways of finding out things I need to know."

I nodded, took a draw off my beer.

"Not two minutes after I heard Ez was dead—I'd barely hung up the phone—your friend Frankie DeNoux called."

I hadn't ever thought of him as my friend, but I guessed now that he must be.

"He told me you'd been taken to the police station and were being held there. By that time it was, I don't know, maybe four in the morning. Frankie was concerned and wanted to know if I could do anything, find out anything."

"So Mr. Frankie knows about you and Miss Dupuy."

"Mr. Frankie. I don't think I've heard that since I left Mississippi. No, he doesn't know. He only wanted to try to keep you from getting in any deeper, maybe get yourself seriously hurt. He called me because I'm someone who can usually find out what's going on and sometimes even get things done."

"You two are tight?"

"There's history between us."

"So then what did you do, threaten a front-page exposé? Unfair treatment of blacks? Hardly news in this city. Or anywhere else, come to think of it."

"Nothing quite that histrionic. I simply picked up the phone and called a judge I know. I explained my concern. He said he'd look into it right away."

"And an hour later I'm out of there."

"More or less."

"Then I owe you my thanks."

"Any debt you might have owed me—had there been one—you'd have repaid this morning."

We finished our beers and walked back up to Louisiana and across. Straughter had parked his blue Falcon a couple of blocks from the house, before a combined laundromat and cleaners. People sat in plastic chairs on the sidewalk out front talking. Steam rose in thick clouds from vents at the back.

"Do you know?" I said. "Do the police have any leads, anything at all?"

"Hard to say. Things are shut up tight on this. But I don't think so."

"Man seems to know what he's doing."

"And he does appear intent upon going ahead with it."

"Do me a favor. Let me know if you hear something?"

Straughter tilted his head to the side and forward, peering at me over rimless glasses. With his chin out like that, I saw how perfectly egg-shaped his head was.

"You wouldn't be taking this personally, would you, Griffin?"

"I don't know how I'm taking it, not yet."

"Just be careful. Don't let it take you instead." He looked up at squirrels chasing one another along a stretch of powerline, chattering furiously. "You read Ez's column yet this morning?"

I nodded. They'd run it on the front page, with her usual picture, alongside the story of her murder and a nighttime shot of the street outside the club where B.R. was playing.

"I still don't understand it, but sometimes that woman knew things nobody else does, things *she* didn't even know she knew. She'd sit down at the typewriter, describe someone, set a scene, and it would all just start coming. She was an uptown girl: Newcomb, sorority, the whole works. What did she know about the life of a black man in prison for murder? But you read the piece. I think the liquor helped make the connections for her at first, whatever the connections were. Later on, she got to like the liquor for itself.''

"She'll be missed.''

"She will be. City won't be the same.'' He held his hand out. "Bullshit. Of course it will be. This city isn't ever anything *but* the same.''

"However hard we try?''

He laughed, we shook hands and parted. I walked back to the house, thinking about Esmé. About my hand reaching out for hers as she mockingly clawed at air, about those fingers falling away from me then, and my slow realization of what had happened.

6.

The woman loving and feeling my care those days was LaVerne. And while I generally made a point of not calling her at work, sometimes an exception shouldered its way in.

I knew her schedule pretty well by then, and got her at the third place I tried. The bartender said just a minute and set the phone down. I listened to what sounded like at least three distinct parties going on in the distance.

"Lewis! Where are you? Are you all right?"

"Fine."

"I know what happened last night. Someone said they thought the police still had you. You sure you're all right?"

"Yeah. They let me go a few hours ago, thanks to a friend."

"Friend?"

"Tell you when I see you. Right now I'm about as dragged out as a man can get."

"So you're at home?"

"Home and heading for Dreamland. How's work?"

"Slow."

"Doesn't sound slow."

"Well. Mostly drinkers. You know. Things'll pick up once lunch's over."

"Come by after while?"

"If I do, honey, it's going to be real late."

"I'll be here."

"Don't wait up for me."

"Real funny, Verne."

I heard a sharp crack, like a shot, in the background. For a moment, everything at that end grew quiet.

"Verne: you okay?"

"I'm fine. Sal just broke his baseball bat across some guy's head that was getting out of hand."

I knew where she was and had to wonder what constituted getting out of hand there. A narrow line, at best. The ruckus had already started up again, louder than before.

"You going to be okay there?"

"I don't know. Hold on, let me check."

She turned away, said something, was back.

"We're in luck, Lew. Sal says it's okay, he has another bat."

We laughed, said good-bye and hung up. I poured half a jelly glass of bourbon from a gallon of K&B. Dragged a chair over by the window and sat with my feet on the sill. The huge old oak tree out there in the yard had been around at least a hundred years. It had seen grand buildings and neighborhoods come and go, seen the city under rule of three different nations. Now it was dying. Birds avoided it. If you touched it, chunks of dry, weightless wood came away, crumbling into your hand, smelling of soil. Soon a hurricane or just a strong wind, or eventually nothing much at all, would bring it crashing down.

I was reading a lot of science fiction back then. I'd drop by a newsstand, pick up a half dozen books and read them all in a couple of days. As that morning edged over into afternoon, I sat by the window sipping bourbon and looking out at the ancient, doomed oak. The big house's back door creaked open and shut as workers hurried home for lunch, students to and from classes. And I found myself thinking about a book I'd read not long ago. *Wasp*, by Eric Frank Russell.

Burrowing in at the lowest levels, a lone man infiltrates a distant world's corrupt society. Through various ruses, surfacing momentarily here and there—an irritant, a catalyst, a wasp—he brings about discord in the governed and invisibly guides them toward revolution.

That seemed a fairly constant theme in the science fiction I read. One man would know what was right, and in the face of great opposition—imprisonment, exile, threats of death, reconditioning—he would change the world. No one seemed to notice that every time one of these far-flung worlds changed, it changed to the very one we were living in. Same values, same taboos, same stratifications.

Americans once believed a single man might change the world. That was what our frontier myths, our stories about rugged individualists, our rough-edged heroes, cowboys, private eyes, were all about. America believed *it* could change the world. Believed this was its destiny.

Now we were ass over head in a war no one could win and after twenty years of waiting for the Big Red Boogie Man to gobble us up at any moment, we'd begun destroying ourselves instead.

No one believed anymore that a single man could change things. Maybe, just maybe, in mass they could. Civil-rights marchers. NAACP, SNCC, SDS. Panthers, Muslims, the Black Hand.

No.

No, I was wrong.

At least one American still truly believed that a single man might change the world.

Last night he had waited in darkness on a roof—for how long? And when Esmé Dupuy and I walked out into the street, he had expressed that belief, given it substance, in sudden action.

7.

I slept ten hours straight and awoke to darkness, disoriented, in a kind of free fall. Esmé Dupuy's face kept receding from me, floating down, away, in absolute silence, blackness closing like water over it. Meanwhile I made my way through a landscape where everything was blurred and indistinct—bushes, trees, the swell of ground, boulders, a pond—and took on form only as I approached. I had all the while a sure sense that someone stood behind me, pacing me precisely, turning as I turned, using my eyes, my consciousness, as one might use a camera.

I lay there listening to traffic pass along Washington, unable to throw off that sense of doubleness even after the rest of the dream had unraveled and spun away.

I reached down to turn on the lamp on the floor by my bed and found a note propped against it.

Lew—
  I was here about 9. You were sleeping so hard I just couldn't stand to wake you up. But I made a pot of coffee and drank a cup of it. The rest of it's for you. Drink it and think about me and I'll talk to you in the morning.

V.

I did both, thought of her and drank the coffee, without milk since what was in the icebox was well on its way to cottage cheesedom.

I thought of the first time I saw her, in a diner one morning around four. I'd just been fired—again—and had woke up with jangled nerves and a pounding thirst from a day-long drunk. She came in wearing a tight blue dress and heels and sat by me and told me she liked my suit. After that, I was there every night. And once a couple of weeks had gone by I asked her to have dinner with me. You mean, like a date? she said.

I finished the coffee and decided to go out to Binx's for a drink.

A forties movie was on the TV over the bar, everything black and dull silver. Both pool tables were being ridden hard. Papa sat at his usual place halfway along the bar. He nodded to me as I sat beside him.

"Lewis. Lost one, I hear." And at my glance went on: "Miss Dupuy. Man getting shot out from beside you, that's not something you forget. Doesn't matter it's in France or your backyard, soldier or civilian."

I nodded. Binx brought me a bourbon and when I pointed at Papa's glass, hit him again too. It wasn't the kind of place they often bothered serving up new glasses. Binx just grabbed the bottle by the neck and poured what looked to be about the right amount into Papa's glass.

"Generous thanks to both you excellent gentlemen," Papa said.

"That's kind of what I have to wonder, too."

Papa took a sip of vodka. I thought about bees at the mouths of flowers. "What is?"

"Whether he's a civilian or a soldier."

"The shooter, you mean."

"Yeah."

"What kind of rig he using?"

"Paper says a .308-caliber, some special load they don't identify."

"Or can't. Well, that's a pro gun, for sure. Wouldn't be one of the regulars. Not what they're into at all, no profit in it. But strays do wander into the herd. You want, I could ask around."

"I'd appreciate it, Papa."

Before he retired, Papa had spent more than forty years hiring and training mercenaries and funneling them in and out of Latin American countries. What he couldn't find out, no one knew.

I'd met him through a guy named Doo-Wop who made a career of cadging drinks in bars all over town. Doo-Wop was always talking about how he'd been a Navy SEAL or rustled Arabians for a stable over in Waco or once played with Joe Oliver, and for a long time I'd assumed that what he told me about Papa was as made up as all the rest of it. But slowly I'd come to realize that those stories *weren't* made up. They were appropriated from various people Doo-Wop drank with and processed for redistribution. The stories became his stock, his product: he traded them for drinks. And as he told them, Doo-Wop in some way believed they were real about himself. Eventually a group of Mexicans I spent a weekend drinking with at La Casa put me on to Papa's being the genuine article.

Binx was standing at the end of the bar. When he caught my eye, I nodded. He grabbed a bourbon and a vodka bottle, brought them over.

"Fill it up, my good man," Papa said. "Doesn't happen often, but I feel young tonight."

Binx glanced my way. I nodded again.

"You won't be feeling much anything very long, you keep putting this stuff away like that, Papa."

"Seize the moment, my young friend. Seize the moment."

"Seize away, Papa. But then what the fuck you gonna do with it, once you caught it?"

Business taken care of, Binx returned like a good fighter to his corner.

"Give me a few days, Lewis. You want to come by and check with me, I guess. Since you don't seem to live anywhere, near as anyone can tell."

"That be okay?"

"I'll be here."

I left enough on the bar for another couple of doubles, threw back the rest of my bourbon and stood.

"You ever hear Big Joe Williams, Lewis?"

"Yeah. Man couldn't tune up a guitar to save his life."

"Once said how all these youngsters, white kids of course, are always asking him how to get inside the blues. You heard this before?"

I shook my head.

"Said the whole point was to get *outside*. Outside the sixteen to

James Sallis

eighteen hours you have to work every day—if you can find work at all. Outside where you have to live and what you and your children have to look forward to. Outside the blue devils that are everywhere you go, that are in everything you do, and aren't ever going to leave you alone.''

Papa turned back around on his stool. He took another gentle sip at his vodka. I remembered what Esmé Dupuy had said about O'Carolan and his beloved Irish whiskey kissing one last time.

''You want a man hurts as bad as this one, Lewis, you don't look for him down here with the rest of us. He's been hurting so much for so long that he doesn't think anyone else can hurt that bad, or ever has. So he's already set himself apart from us. Outside. He's gone on to some other level, one where maybe hurt doesn't have anything to do with it any longer. You want to find him, you look *up*.''

I stood there a moment.

Then I said, ''Thank you, Papa.''

8.

I stopped by the apartment to pick up the .38 I carried sometimes back then, before I learned better. A manila envelope was stuffed halfway into the mailbox by my front door. Hosie Straughter's name and address had been marked off and LEW scrawled above in what looked like crayon. Inside was a book, *The Stranger*, and a note in pencil on a piece of paper torn from a grocery sack.

> Thanks again, Griffin. This is one of my
> favorites—by way of appreciation. This
> copy's been mine a long time. Now it's yours.

Since Claiborne was closest, I went there first. Not the smartest thing for a black man to do, start climbing around on roofs at 12:30 in the morning: I'll give you that.

A fire escape began about eight feet up the back of the building, really little more than a steel ladder set sideways and bolted into the bricks. I jumped, caught a rung and scrambled up.

Business was still brisk at the Chick'n Shack half a block uptown. Mostly groups of three or four young men and singles coming home from work, from the look of it. A few cars, but most of them on foot.

Just downtown I could see the Holy Evangelical Church, a single-story brown-brick structure with a stubby spire of multicolored plastic squares and rectangles. The church's windows were painted over black, as were those of Honest Abe's pawnshop (yellow cinderblock)

43

and Lucky Pierre's FaSTop (bare cypress). This was back before the city had bars on every door and window.

Up here, you got a good view of the whole expanse, from Louisiana down at least to Terpsichore, just before the tangle of overpasses and dogleg streets leading into downtown New Orleans. It was the tallest building in the stretch; no one was going to spot you. Downtown buildings might as well be in another state. And you had a choice of flight paths: back down the fire escape or onto one of the adjoining roofs.

He'd chosen the spot carefully.

I squatted at the roof's edge and sighted along an imaginary rifle. He'd have had the strap wound about his right arm for stability, maybe even a small folding tripod. High-resolution scope. Instead of tracking, he'd extrapolate the movement of his subject and sight in on where the subject *would* be, waiting for him to step into place. Hold his breath instinctively when that happened. Squeeze. Breathe out.

I caught the merest glimmer of what it must have been like, a momentary connection far more emotional than intellectual, then it was gone. So much for blinding insight, for sudden epiphanies that change your life.

Starting back down the fire escape, I heard voices below. Two men about my age stood by my car, one of those Galaxies with the bat-wing rear ends. The taller guy held a strip of flexible metal with a notch at the end. The shorter one held a brick. They were in conference.

"You gentlemen manage on your own, or you need help?"

"Keep on walking, man." The tall one.

"None of *yo'* business."

I shook my head sadly. "Unmistakable mark of the amateur. Never willing to take advantage of the resources available. Always has to do things the hard way."

"Yeah. Well, I'll ama *yo'* teur."

"Man, what the fuck you—"

He stopped because I'd stepped in and slammed my fist into his gut and he just couldn't bring himself to go on. He went down instead. I grabbed the homemade Slim Jim as it went by and whacked it against the other one's head. It made a singing sound. The short guy's brick skidded into the street where a White Fleet Cab lurched over it. Something, possibly an elbow, cracked as he went down.

I transferred funds, a couple hundred, from their pockets to my wallet, then unlocked the Ford, got in and fired it up, heading for Jefferson Avenue.

Half the apartment complex there dated from the early fifties, textured stucco, French windows and medallions everywhere. The rest, a lower structure of interconnected wooden bungalowlike apartments, had been tacked on more recently: a kind of fanciful sidecar. All of it according to *The Times-Picayune* had been shut down for almost a year now. Funding had run out with renovation well under way. Balconies and entryways drooped in disrepair, bare two-by-fours showed in cavities where facades had been hammered partly through, piles of old lumber, flooring and plasterboard lay moldering in the yard and parking lot.

On the right, an empty double lot stretched to the street corner. The other side looked down on a row of shotgun cottages. Across the street a small park with swing sets and picnic tables fronted a wooden fence and a line of identical condos each painted a different pastel.

No easy access this time. I climbed a young elm and dropped onto a tarpaper roof awash in detritus. Beer bottles, scraps of roofing, remains of packing crates and take-out meals, bits of cast-off vegetation, clothing, cardboard, bits of cast-off lives. Near the back, however, in a kind of corridor formed by a sealed chimney and heating vent, all was in order. Against one end where these met, someone had propped a massive old door. Over it, a slab of plywood served as roof. Beneath were a legless chair, burned-down candles in coffee cans, scorched saucepans, a huddle of sheets and thin curtains torn into rags. A square of bricks stacked two deep, ash and chunks of wood burned to a weightless white heap within.

Nothing to connect it with the sniper, of course. The city was full of such desperate islands. Abandoned houses, boarded-up cafés and corner grocery stores, the culverts of open canals. Obviously the police didn't think there was any direct connection. If they had, these things would have been carted off as evidence.

All the same, it definitely looked as though someone had been living here. And while I kept telling myself it could have been anyone, myself wasn't paying much attention to me.

I climbed down a drainpipe at the building's streetside corner, then sat in the car a while going over what I had learned.

The reason it took so long was that I hadn't learned anything, so I just kept going over it all again and again. But when you're stuck, it doesn't much matter how hard you rev the engine and spin the wheels. You have to find something solid. A board, a branch. Jam it in there, hit the gas once more, and you're moving.

Maybe myself had the board and was just keeping it out of sight.

In which case I couldn't do much besides wait him out—so I might as well get on with business.

Having little inclination to revisit Dryades just yet, I drove down LaSalle to Loyola and headed on into downtown New Orleans. Parked in front of the telephone office on Poydras and walked up to Baronne. Not much traffic except for cabs. And while the Quarter would still be bustling, things *this* side of Canal were pretty much deserted. The few people I encountered strode purposefully along, staying well out on the sidewalk, keeping watch about them.

I looked up. Toward the top of a mock-gothic office building, The Stanhope, with brass-clad revolving door and tiled, bright lobby at street level. Toward the crest of an art deco hotel hashed (judging from signs on windows) into a copy shop, dance studio, commercial photographer, credit union, tailor. It had to be one of those two buildings. But after half an hour of searching I couldn't find any way of getting up either of them.

I did find an unsuspected narrow alleyway running between buildings, like a chink in rock, toward Carondelet and the site of the second killing.

I was maybe halfway through when I heard a shot, a small-caliber pistol from the sound of it, ahead of me.

I inched out into halflight and stood there scarcely breathing. My own blood hammered at my ears.

Voices.

No: a single voice.

Too low, too far off, for me to make out what it was saying. In another alleyway like this one?

Then something moved, shadow settling back into shadow, across Carondelet, in a cleft between buildings. Nothing there when I watched now: had I really seen it? That was where the sound came from.

Courting shade and shadow myself, I eased into the street. A cab swung onto Carondelet a block away, headlights like two lances, a death ray, and I froze. This was how rabbits and deer felt. But almost immediately the cab turned off. I made it across unseen, and with my back pressed against brick beside the cul-de-sac could hear what was being said.

"Man just can't keep to himself anymore, can't be left alone. You've been on me for a while. And not because you *believe* in something. That would be all right. But it's only because I'm a bootstrap you think you can use to pull yourself up. Now look: you've found me. Pure Borges. The hunter becomes prey. Poor great white hunter."

Hands flat on the wall, I leaned to my right to peer cautiously around the corner. Remembering the periscope, a yellow cardboard tube with two cheap mirrors, I'd bought at Kress's for ninety-nine cents when I was twelve. One man stood over another. This man, lean, dark, was talking. He held a small revolver loosely alongside one leg, in his left hand. The other man lay slumped against the wall, both hands pressed into his groin. A darkish patch of blood beneath him.

"We all know what's right. Part of what we're born with. Body goes against that, it only starts to destroy itself."

The man slumped against the wall said something I couldn't make out.

"I know," the other one said, raising the gun. "I'm sorry. Never was any good with these things. I didn't intend to hurt you, it should have been quick."

Holding the .38 two-handed, I stepped into the mouth of the cul-de-sac.

"Don't do it!" I said, just as someone behind *me* said, "What the fuck!"

Reflexively I turned. A middle-aged man stood there in the street holding a baseball bat.

"Don't guess *you* were the guys called a cab, huh?"

I spun back around in time to see the shooter scrambling over a dumpster and through a delivery door behind it. I got off a couple of rounds before I even realized I was firing. One of them rang against the dumpster's steel. The other hit the door just as it closed.

Then everything went black.

Someone stood over me. Something struck at my back, something thudded into a kidney, deflected off an elbow. Someone said "Goddam niggers ... Used to be a fine city ... Teach this one a lesson anyway." I knew it was happening, but I didn't feel the blows. I'd gone away. I was floating above it all, looking down.

Fragments drifted up to me.

It. Down. Now.

Can't. A white man. Got to.

Don't be. Deep. Enough.

A broad face loomed above mine. Curly dark-blond hair. Face ashine with sweat. I was pretty sure it was the guy who'd been slumped against the wall. I could smell garlic on his breath.

"Hang on," he said. "You're okay. There's an ambulance on the way."

"You the one's been whacking at me?" I said.

"No. He's taken care of."

"Glad to hear it. *You* okay? Looked like a lot of blood."

"I'm fine. And alive, thanks to you."

"Things gonna get better soon."

"We all hope so."

"I mean it." Darkness was closing on me, rushing in like water at the edge of the frame.

"We all mean it. Meanwhile, better let me have the gun."

I didn't realize I was still holding on to it.

"I'm a cop," he said. "Don Walsh."

And the water closed over me.

9.

In May of 1967, on a dry, lifeless Sacramento day, members of the Black Panther Party from the San Francisco Bay area converged on the California state legislature with M-1 rifles and 12-gauge shotguns cradled in their arms, .45-caliber pistols and cartridge belts at their waists.

Newspapers and broadcasts all over the country gave feature coverage to the Sacramento "armed invasion."

The Party had come to announce its opposition to a bill severely restricting public carriage of loaded weapons. Since this was not prohibited under current law, the police were impelled to return the weapons they'd begun confiscating from the Panthers in the corridors outside the legislative chamber. Eventually eighteen Party members were arrested on charges of disrupting the state legislature (a misdemeanor) and conspiracy to disrupt the state legislature (a felony). Conspiracy was big back then.

The Panthers weren't in fact particularly interested in whether or not the gun bill passed. They'd continue to own and carry weapons, visibly, legally or not. Their real purpose was to direct media attention, *people's* attention, to the fact that blacks in ghettos had little recourse *but* armed self-defense.

They were expressing the desperation and anger of a people pushed aside and set against themselves, a desperation and anger no civil-rights legislation or social program had ever touched or was likely to.

I watched the Sacramento confrontation on TV within hours of its happening, in a bar on Magazine, five or six Scotches into what became a long evening.

Years before, during the course of the events I'm putting down here, I'd gone with Hosie Straughter to hear a black American novelist living in Paris give a talk at Dillard on a rare U.S. visit. Reading passages from his books, he said that slavery, discrimination and racial hatred, even poverty, were only the first steps toward the destruction of a people: the final one was the terrible, irrevocable damage his people were now doing to one another.

I thought of Sacramento and of that novelist again just yesterday—almost thirty years later—as I sat in the Downtown Joy on Canal watching *Boyz N the Hood.*

So much time has gone by. So little has changed.

10.

As I lay there, various faces—Frankie DeNoux, LaVerne, Hosie Straughter, anonymous doctors and nurses—hovered in the sky above me.

Howya feelin', Lewis?

Anything at all, you let me know, you hear?

Look like you gone home to Arkansas and ol' Faubus done got hold of you.

Contusions.

Multiple lacerations.

Mild concussion.

May be cervical damage.

Those last four items (I was pretty sure) from the same source, and oddly chantlike, as though someone far off were singing "the hip bone's connected to the thigh bone, the thigh bone's connected to the ..." and so on. With that little hiccough just before the new bone gets mentioned.

Afterward, asleep, awake and at a hundred bus stops somewhere in between, I listened to the words, the chants, go on rolling and unrolling in my head.

Contusions. Multiple lacerations. Mild concussion. May be cervical damage.

Conlacerations, mild latusions, maybe cause multiple dams, vehicle damn age.

I remember trying to talk to those faces hovering up there above

51

me. Maybe I did talk to them, I don't know, don't know what I might have said if I did. I don't even know if they were really there. I was afloat on a chemical raft. Faces, towns, states, shores, years went by.

Someone stood over me saying there was someone he wanted me to meet. It was important that we talked. But then a wind came up, or a current, and I wasn't there anymore. I wasn't anywhere. It was great.

A few more faces and months went by.

Actually, the whole thing lasted only five or six hours—as I discovered when the drugs started easing off to make way for the pain. They made a *lot* of room, I want to tell you. And unlike most other New Orleans real estate, it didn't go vacant long.

Someone was saying: "Jesus, you look worse than I do. I'd have bet good money that wasn't possible."

I asked what time it was. A clock hung on the wall across from me, but wayward and unfocusing as my eyes were, it could as well have been a fish tank.

Some time after six, he said. Sure enough: scratchy dawn at the window. My cruise down life, time, and the river hadn't been such a long one after all.

He leaned close.

"Remember me?"

I nodded. "You okay?"

"Yeah, but I wouldn't of been if you hadn't happened along. Bullet went through. Lots of blood, hurt like a sunuvabitch, but no real damage."

I looked at the heavy bandage strapped around his thigh. To make room for it, they'd cut the pant leg off, so he's wearing a sportcoat, shirt and tie, black socks and shoes, and his bare hairy leg's hanging out there in the wind.

"You look ridiculous."

"Guess it depends on your perspective. Like most things. Compared to what I was *expecting* to look like for a while there, this is great, believe me."

He held out his hand. It was wide, pink, and grimy. Traces of blood still around the nails and under them.

Unaccustomed to shaking hands with whites, I hesitated, then took it.

"Don Walsh."

"I'm—"

"I know. Robert Lewis Griffin, but you don't use the first name. And I don't believe I've *ever* been as pleased to make a new acquaintance."

We laughed. It hurt.

"So you okay, Lewis? Get you anything?"

"Out of here."

"Not quite yet. But the doctors say everything goes all right, it's just overnight."

"Then what?"

"Whatever you want, good buddy."

"I'm not under arrest?"

"Not hardly. Hell, Lewis, you're a hero. Save one more cop's life, they'll make you citizen of the year."

"But the gun—"

"Was fired twice by an officer of the law, with due and proper warning, at a suspect fleeing arrest."

"You're kidding."

"Far as anyone knows, far as anyone's *going* to know, that gun was mine. All you did was come to the assistance of a wounded police officer."

I was silent.

"What?" he said.

"Just thinking. Thing like that gets out on the street, it's all over for me."

He watched my face for several moments. Clear green eyes flecked with gold.

"It's a whole different world isn't it, the one you live in?"

I nodded.

"Yeah." He got up and limped to the window, stood there looking out. Light filled it now. "It's hard to remember that sometimes, hard to understand."

"I bet."

He turned back. "Look. Nothing's been fed to the press yet. You want, no one outside the department has to hear anything about this."

"You can do that?"

"I can try." He came back over to the bed and put his hand out again. "Thank you, Lewis. I mean that. I'm lucky you happened by."

"I didn't just happen by."

He looked closely at me.

"That was the shooter, right?"

He nodded.

"I was looking for him."

"Yeah," he said after a moment. "Yeah, I figured. But no one else has to know about that, either."

A nurse came in to take vital signs and see if I needed anything. She had pale skin, red hair. I thanked her as she left.

Walsh said: "You get out of here, Lewis, I'm taking you for the best steak dinner you ever had."

"Take me along, you're gonna find it cuts into your choice of places."

"There is that." He grinned. "Might just have to put cuffs on you and tell 'em you're in custody."

"You're a desperate man."

"Take care, Lewis."

He started out.

"You never mentioned what *you* were doing there," I said.

He turned back. "Same thing as you. The bus driver that got shot on Carondelet?"

I nodded.

"That was my brother."

11.

We settled on breakfast. I still owe you that steak dinner then, Walsh told me. You don't owe me one damn thing, I told him.

I was awake, out of bed and dressed when the nurse came in at six. It was still mostly dark outside, light nibbling at the sky's borders in the window.

You're supposed to be in bed, Mr. Griffin.

Do I need to sign anything on my way out?

Administration's not open till eight.

That could be a problem.

I'd have to call the resident on duty, probably the administrator too.

Please.

I have a lot of things that need taking care of, Mr. Griffin, lots of other patients to see.

I'm sure you do.

She sighed.

I never saw the resident or administrator on call. But six brusque phone conversations later I pushed open the front doors of Touro to find Walsh waiting at the curb in his blue Corvair.

"Need a lift, sailor? Steak dinner perhaps?"

"Little early for dinner, you think?"

He shrugged. "Always dinnertime *some*where."

In the car I asked him how he knew when I'd be leaving. He said he had me figured for the kind who'd try to slip through the crack of dawn. Patience not being a particular virtue of yours, he said. Or mine either for that matter, he added after a moment.

He cut over to St. Charles heading downtown.

"Breakfast be okay, for now?" he asked, and when I said sure, he hauled the little car into the neutral ground for a U-turn back up toward Napoleon. We pulled into the K&B there just as I was telling him he didn't owe me a thing.

The breakfast special, three eggs, bacon, grits and biscuit, coffee included, was $1.49. But first we had to sit at an empty table a while waiting. Walsh finally got up, went over and spoke to the waitress behind the counter, who'd been pointedly ignoring us. She almost beat him back to the table with coffee and menus, and a broad smile, for us both. *Sallye*, her nametag said.

"Funny the things you just never think about," he said as she walked away.

"The ones you try *not* to think about are a scream, too."

Food was there by the time we finished our coffee. The waitress slid plates in front of us and hurried off to bring more coffee in thick-walled mugs. She took the old ones away. Grits swam with bright butter, bacon glistened with grease, eggs were a yellow dam dividing grits grease from bacon grease. Even the bottom of the biscuit was soaked with butter. Mmmmmm.

"Sure you can afford this?" I asked.

"Don't worry. I've been saving up for it."

The minute we were done, the waitress was back bringing new mugs of coffee and carrying off plates, asking did we need anything else. Walsh shook his head. Sallye left.

"What the hell did you say to that woman?"

"Told her you were an African, taught economics up at Tulane."

"You didn't."

"No. I didn't. I just said I was a police officer and that we'd appreciate some breakfast after a real tough night's work. It's possible she may have gotten the impression that you're a cop too, I suppose."

We sat sipping coffee, watching streetcars and people lumber by outside, trading what little we knew about the shooter.

Walsh had made a point of spending as much time as possible these past weeks in the vicinity of the shooting sites.

"I'd swing by whenever I could when I was on patrol, dog them

on my own after hours. There was this one guy wearing all black—
T-shirt, jeans, some kind of short jacket, maybe canvas, with a lot
of pockets—I caught a glimpse of a couple or three times. Always
from the back, always just for an instant as he was heading down
an alley or cutting between buildings. But I knew from the walk it
had to be the same guy.

"Then one night, heading up toward Lee Circle from downtown,
I saw him, someone that walked like him anyway, coming out of
the Hummingbird. I was in the unit and didn't want to spook him,
so by the time I was able to pull around a corner and get out, the
guy was already gone down Julia Street somewhere. But that put the
Hummingbird at the top of my hit list. I started spending time in a
low-life bar across St. Charles drinking draft beer that smelled like
cleaning fluid and tasted like sour water. Then yesterday morning, I
put my beer down, looked out the window between some old cardboard signs, and there he was.

"We went together down Julia and up Baronne. Nothing but bars
and a few fleabag hotels open, the rest of the street empty, so I'm
hanging way the hell back. But somehow he got on to me. Knew I
was there, knew I'd been tracking him."

"And decided to stop you."

"Right."

"Any way he could know who you are?"

"I don't think so. You ready? She's looking this way again with
coffee in her eyes."

Walsh put a five on the table and we limped together out to his car.

"Where's home?"

I must have looked at him sharply.

"I just meant that I'll drop you."

"Which way you going?"

He hooked a thumb toward uptown.

"Good enough. You can let me off at State."

"You sure?"

I told him I was sure, and told him the same thing again, leaning
down to the window, once I got out at State.

There's this house there on the corner with a glassed-in porch and
artificial Christmas tree. Only it isn't a Christmas tree, it's a Whatever tree. Stays up year round. Come Easter, pink bunnies and huge
plastic eggs appear on it. Halloween, they decorate it with skeletons

and spiders, witches, spray-on webs. Masks, streamers, and clowns go up for Mardi Gras. Now it was hung with turkeys, Indians, cranberry bunches, Pilgrim hats.

I stood for a moment wondering (as I had wondered a hundred times before) about the people who lived in that house, what they were like, why they did this, how it all got started. This is a city that dearly loves traditions, and if there's not one handy, then it'll just make up a new one.

I crossed St. Charles and walked riverward toward LaVerne's place.

No mail in the box, of course, no paper on the porch or in the yard: Verne was almost as invisible as I was.

I let myself in, poured half a tumblerful of bourbon in the kitchen, and took it into the front room.

At the time, Verne had a taste for what they called the contemporary look. You'd walk into her second-floor apartment in this old Victorian house and there, sitting on hardwood floors alongside real plaster walls and solid-wood baseboards under cameo-and-wreath ceiling medallions, was all this stark, angular, mostly white furniture. It remained kind of a shock.

Not too long after, Verne switched to (and stayed with) old wooden tables, breakfronts, wardrobes and chairs picked up for next to nothing at used-furniture shops on Magazine and hauled upstairs over the balcony on ropes. One day she arrived breathless to tell me that all the stores had tripled their prices and put up new signs and now she had an apartment full of fine antiques.

Finishing my drink, I poked through books and magazines scattered about on the coffee table. *Life*, several Mentor Classics, something titled *The Killer Inside Me*, an Ace Double with a Philip K. Dick novel on the A side, *Redbook*, *Family Circle*, a paperback of *Butterfield 8* with Elizabeth Taylor on the cover.

I opened *Life* to a spread on Hemingway that, along with half a dozen older photos, included one of him standing outside his home in Idaho just days before he shot himself with one of his beloved shotguns. Was there snow in the background? I remember snow.

I went to the kitchen for another drink. Wandered out onto the balcony, careful to stay back out of direct sight of the street.

A fire burned somewhere close by. I could smell it: loamy, full aroma of wood, acrid tang of synthetics and fabric, heat itself.

Second time I was ever at LaVerne's, letting myself in with a key same as now, I walked out on this balcony with a cup of *café au lait* and within ten minutes cops were banging on the door below. When I answered it, they threw me up against the wall shouting *What you doin' here, boy? You belong here?* Luckily Verne's neighbor heard it all and told her when she got home in the morning. So four hours after I was hauled in, Verne showed up at police headquarters with her lawyer. Details run together from incident to incident, year to year, but I think I emerged from that particular instance of "cooperation" (no record of arrest, of course) with a fractured rib, broken finger, multiple abrasions. All preexisting, of course. You *know* how them darkies live.

It didn't look as though Verne was coming home—not all that unusual. Maybe she'd sold an overnight, or she was staying with one of her regulars. So I had a couple more drinks, napped a bit in front of the TV, and some time after noon walked over to catch the streetcar down to Washington.

Hosie Straughter stood up from the stoop in front of my house as I came around the wall.

12.

"Lewis. You look like absolute unmitigated hell."

"That's the trouble with you journalists. Always leaping headfirst for the nearest cliché. You have any idea how many times I've already heard that?"

"Women and little children scream and run when they see you, I guess."

"Women, anyway."

"Know how that is. You okay?"

"I will be. I think. Some time around January, maybe. Late January."

"Barring further complications."

"There is that."

"But from what I know, seems to me the complications so far didn't come find *you*, you went looking for *them*."

"Leaping for another cliché?"

"Or jumping to conclusions: you better believe it. With both bare feet. But I'm looking around close and hard as I come down."

"Yeah. Yeah, you would be. Want some coffee?"

"Only if you hold a gun on me. I was up all night working, already had nine, ten cups."

"A drink, then?"

"Wouldn't mind. Only had five or six of those."

So we went in and I rinsed two of the glasses on the counter by the sink and poured Scotch into them. We sat at the kitchen table.

In the South that's where all the best talking gets done. I put the bottle between us on the table and asked Hosie what he knew.

"Well. I never had doubt one that you'd be going after this person, of course. Couldn't tell, though, whether it would be right away, or later. I already knew from something Frankie told me, once I put it together with a couple other things I'd caught here and there on the streets, that this young patrolman, guy named Walsh, had the same gleam in his eye. So last night when both your names come up in conversation—after I call from the paper to inquire the nature and extent of your injuries—I pretty much know what's happened. I just don't have any particulars. And in my line of work, particulars are the only things *worth* having."

He settled back with his glass resting on one leg, an actor who had delivered his lines and now could coast.

"I'm afraid that's about as particular as it gets," I told him. "We don't know who the shooter is, don't know anything about him, really. Walsh was dogging the places shootings had occurred. He kept seeing this guy. Knew him from the way he walked. I was chasing shadows too, and one of the shadows jumped up to become a guy holding a gun on Walsh."

Hosie had a sip of Scotch. "I don't know whether to call that incredible luck, or astonishing stupidity."

"You got me. Wrong place, right time?"

He grunted. "So that was it, huh? Your wad's shot. Blank slate, start all over again, same as before."

"Yeah. Except now he knows we're out here, of course."

"So he'll be harder to find. . . . He doesn't know who you are, right? Either of you?"

"We don't think he does."

Hosie stared at the tabletop while I looked out the window at squirrels chasing one another across power lines. When I found my glass empty, I refilled both.

"That's good," he said. I never knew if he meant the refill or the shooter's not knowing who we were. Because just then the door opened and we both looked toward it.

"Lew. You okay? I went straight home once I heard what happened. Thought you'd be there."

"I was."

"You ever give any thought to maybe leaving a note, let someone know you're all right?"

I stood and hugged her. She felt wonderful, smelled wonderful, the way she always did. She was wearing a short blue dress, shiny and satinlike, with red heels (pumps, she called them) and huge red earrings.

"Hosie, this is LaVerne."

"It sure is."

"Verne: Hosie Straughter. He's—"

"I know." She held out her hand. "Truly a pleasure, Mr. Straughter. I've enjoyed your writing over the years, and learned so much from it."

"Lewis," he said, cupping their joined hands with his free one. "This is *not* what one would call a fine Scotch. In fact, more discerning drinkers might be disinclined to call it a Scotch at all. And your attire, this horrid black suit gone slick at the knees, with its uneven cuffs: also questionable. But, be all that as it may, I am forced to admit that your taste in *friends* is ... exemplary. Unassailable. Absolutely. The pleasure, young lady," he said, lowering his head, "is entirely mine, believe me."

He picked up his glass and drank off the couple of inches I'd just poured. "And with that simple, heartfelt toast, I'll leave you two young people to whatever it is that young people do these days."

Over my protests he left, and we had indeed set about doing what young people did those days, when someone knocked at the door.

"Lewis! You in there?"

"Hang on." I stood up, straightened things and looked at Verne. She made a face and straightened her own things.

I opened the door a few inches. He wore black jeans, western boots, a yellow Ban-Lon shirt. Squinting in the bright sunlight.

"What are you doing here? And more important, how did you find me?"

"Hope you don't mind. Figured after you got some sleep—"

"Which hasn't happened yet."

"—we could get together and—"

He stopped, jaw still working. "Hey. I'm sorry. You get to bed." At which point LaVerne stepped into sight. "I can come back."

I opened the door the rest of the way.

"Better come on in. Sun shining off your white face like that, down here, it's liable to blind someone. You want coffee? Nice shirt, by the way."

"Had a potful of it already. Hello, miss." His eyes went back and forth between us a couple of times.

"LaVerne: Don Walsh." They both nodded. "A drink, then?"

"You got a beer?"

I did. I tracked it down in the icebox, trapped it, and handed it to him. He rolled the first mouthful around a while, swallowed.

"There's this guy over on Jackson keeps an eye and ear open for us."

"A snitch." So I wasn't as invisible as I thought I was. We seldom are.

"Yeah, well, what's in a name. He's turned a lot of things our way."

"Including my address."

"It's any consolation to you, I did have to tell him exactly what our connection was."

"We don't *have* a connection, Officer."

Silence shimmered in the air like heat lightning.

"I'll be going now, Lew," Verne said. "It's been a long night. Get some sleep, call me later on?"

"You need a cab?"

"No, honey. St. John gave me a lift." *Sinjun.* Her fifty-year-old neighbor who still dressed in chinos, sweater, blue shirt, loafers. Like many people in this city, he seemed stuck, like a fly in amber, in some prior era. "He's waiting at a bar on Claiborne."

"Beautiful woman," Walsh said.

True enough. Heads turned, men's and women's alike, wherever she went, and I was pleased, flattered, *proud*, to have her beside me. Only much later, after almost thirty years with and without her, and when it was too late, did I realize that LaVerne had saved my life—that in some strange, indecipherable way we had saved each other's lives.

And in the years before that realization came, without meaning to I would hurt her terribly again and again, the same way I'd repeatedly damage myself. Each year, the ground pulls harder. Each year, the burden of what we do and fail to do helps push us down.

"You want another beer?" I said. "No? Then what the hell *do* you want?"

"A question I've asked myself again and again."

"Ever get an answer?"

"Oh yes. Lots of them."

He found the trashcan under the sink and dropped the bottle in.

"I want to stop feeling this hole where my brother was. I want things to make sense. I want justice and truth and decency and clear blue skies."

"Walsh?"

"Yeah?"

"You're going to have a miserable life, man."

13.

We found him, casting ourselves bodily for the fifth or sixth time into the abyss of the absurdly hopeful, ready to call it quits after one, two more, tops, at a bar not far off Lee Circle on Girod.

He had on a tuxedo coat with lapels wide as mud flaps, purple-and-green Hawaiian shirt, khaki work pants, hightop tennis shoes with most of the black worn away. There were patches on the pants that looked like they belonged on a tire.

"Looking good, Doo-Wop."

"Captain." Doo-Wop was able to recall the minutest detail of a story you told him four years ago, but he couldn't remember your name from the beginning of a sentence to its end; so everyone was captain. "Been a while."

"This is Walsh."

"Captain," he said.

Walsh nodded.

"We're looking for someone."

"Course you are."

I laid a five on the bar. It vanished as quickly as a fly landing by a lizard. First step.

Then the second. "A bourbonish afternoon, I believe," he said.

So I ordered a round. Paying the toll. The bourbon came out of a jug, but the way Doo-Wop sampled it, it might have been a twenty-year-old single malt. He put the glass down and turned to look at me, ready for business.

I told him we didn't have much to go on. Told him where Walsh had seen the guy, time of day, how he'd been dressed. Walsh even tried to copy his walk, a deliberate, measured gait: feet placed straight and parallel, toe coming down before heel.

"That's not it," he said, "but it's close. Arms at his sides. They don't move as he walks. Come to think of it, nothing much seems to move *but* his feet."

Doo-Wop thought it over. "Maybe," he said. He had another little taste of bourbon and put the glass down empty. I signaled to have it refilled. He nodded acknowledgment of the transaction. "Joint on St. Peters. Twice, if it's your man."

"When?" Walsh said.

Doo-Wop just looked at him.

"Doo-Wop kind of lives on Hopi Mean Time," I explained. "Everything's in the present."

Walsh nodded.

"This guy ever with anybody else?" I asked. "Or ever seem to know anybody there?"

Doo-Wop shook his head. "Sits by himself. Has a beer, two. Leaves. Don't talk or want to."

"You tried."

"Slow night. I was thirsty."

"It was night, then. Dark."

"Yeah. Must of been. Streetlights have this kind of shell around them. Wouldn't be there days."

"Cold?"

"Well, I'm wearing what I've got on now. So it can't be all that warm."

I ordered another round, but by his own reckoning and standards, apparently, Doo-Wop had drunk an amount of whiskey equal to the information he was able to provide. The new bourbon stood untouched before him. Walsh and I started in on ours.

"Captain," he said eventually.

I turned to him.

"I have a story to tell you."

"Fair enough."

"You decide if it's worth anything."

I nodded.

What follows is not what Walsh and I heard then, a stuttering, inchoate tale in which the narrator seemed at times a participant, and which seemed somehow still to be going on, but a version pieced together from Doo-Wop's story and a subsequent telephone conversation with Frankie DeNoux.

For three or four years a building at Dryades and Terpsichore has served as clubhouse, schoolroom, barracks, refuge and halfway house—though officially listed in city records as a temple. It's headquarters for a group calling itself Yoruba. The group's minister and family live there, along with others.

Yoruba has gained considerable influence in its immediate community over time and has slowly extended that influence into surrounding communities. Highly visible in their plain cotton clothing dyed light purple, Yoruba's members devote themselves to community service: caring for the young so that parents might work, staffing referral and health-care services, volunteering as teachers and teachers' assistants, reading to children at makeshift storefront libraries or to shut-ins at home and in medical facilities.

Yoruba's sole income derives from the tithes of its followers and from the contributions of other well-wishers. Each Friday these "operating funds" are gathered at various collection sites and delivered to the temple by Yoruba's minister of defense, Jamil Xtian.

For three, four years this has gone on, no problem. But last Friday there's someone waiting there by the back door. Two average-height, average-weight men in nondescript clothes and Mardi Gras masks. They step out from behind hedges by the steps and say, We'll take that off your hands.

When Xtian reaches for his gun, they shoot him once through the chest and grab the duffel bag stuffed with cash. And by the time others come pouring out of the house, all of them trained fighters and all of them armed, the two are gone.

Gone with, according to word on the street, somewhere between ten and fifteen thousand dollars.

"That's it," Doo-Wop said.

I put a twenty on the bar, ordered another round. The twenty vanished. Dipping his head a couple of degrees, Doo-Wop acknowledged payment in full. He sampled the new pouring. Approved it.

I looked at Walsh.

He shrugged.

"Could be. There's definitely been a buzz, *something* going on.

No report, but then there probably wouldn't be. And if someone did report it, that's *all* we'd get.''

"This couldn't have anything to do with the guy we're looking for.''

"Anything direct, you mean.''

"Right.''

"Don't see how.''

"Hang tight. I'll be back.''

I asked after the phone and found it in the men's room clinging to a narrow wall between urinal and sink. Dropped in my nickel and dialed Frankie DeNoux.

I'm sure I only imagined the sound of teeth sinking into chicken at the other end. And the sound of a cardboard tray being set down, grease oozing slowly out onto files, correspondence, briefs.

"Griffin,'' I said. "I need some help.''

"You got it.''

An elderly man came out of the stall, washed his hands at the sink and, turning to get a paper towel from the stack, splattered soapy water on my shoes. I flattened myself against the wall so he could get out.

"Something on the street. Started last Friday, Saturday.''

"People in purple involved?''

"Seems so.''

"And some others in black shirts and berets.''

"Hadn't heard that part.''

Frankie told me what he knew, then listened to what I'd been able to figure out from Doo-Wop's story.

"So who's wearing the funny hats?'' I asked.

"Who always wears them? The elect, the preterite. Those who know what's best for all of us—even when the rest of us don't.''

"Why aren't the police on this?''

"You're kiddin' me—right, Lew?''

Another man came into the restroom, looked around briefly, and left.

"There's no way the police are gonna get notified. Who's gonna trust them, something like this? Better listen to Malcolm, brother. Negroes have to solve their own problems. We can't expect white society to.''

"Man, you run errands for one of the worst parts of white society. We both do."

"Yeah. Well, chicken's cheap, but it ain't *that* cheap."

"You're telling me the Yoruba theft's internal."

"Mmm-hmm."

"Blacks ripping off other blacks."

"Way I see it, sure."

"A power play of some kind? Something territorial?"

"Could be. It's an old song, Lew. But I'll ask around."

"Thanks. I'll be in touch."

When I got back to the bar, Walsh had bought Doo-Wop a drink and was talking to him. Years later, in another bar, I heard Doo-Wop telling someone else who'd bought him a drink about the time he'd been a cop.

14.

With the work I did, how I lived, there's no way I was going to keep regular hours. I didn't keep hours at all. They just loomed around me and passed by like Carnival floats. But my course through days and nights had zigzagged a lot worse than usual that past week or so, and maybe it was starting to wear me down.

Walsh and I walked out of the bar into streets suspended timelessly somewhere between dark and light. Everything was either blinding white or dead black, edges leached away by gray—like in old movies. For a moment I didn't know if it was morning or evening. And for another terrifying moment I had no idea where I was.

Then Walsh's hand fell on my shoulder and it all began settling back in place.

"I've got to get some sleep," I said.

"Know what you mean."

We walked back to his car, in one of those narrow downtown lots that look like they'll hold maybe eight cars, but the attendants have twenty of them lined up in there.

"Talk to you later," I said.

"The hell you will. Get in the car, Lewis."

"I'm going to walk. Clear my head."

"Man thinks he's at the beach."

"Then I better be watching where I step."

Walsh laughed.

A plane had gone down in Lake Pontchartrain months back, and stories of swimmers treading on disembodied heads as they waded into high water were all the rage. Supposedly this had led to temporary closure of the beach. But the real problem was pollution, all the sewage and industrial waste we'd dumped into the lake. Authorities went on playing open-and-shut for years before they finally closed the beach down. I always wondered what happened to all the rides and buildings they had out there.

I held my hand up, touched finger briefly to forehead, and started off toward Poydras. Watching where I stepped.

Carborne, on bus, on foot, and trolleyback, people were whooshing out of the business district like air from a punctured balloon.

I turned up Magazine and walked along slowly, realizing that this one spinning about me now was a world, a life, I'd never know. Homes and families to go back to or leave, regular jobs, paychecks, routines, appointments, security. A fish's life would hardly be more alien to me. I didn't know what that said about me, I didn't know how I felt about it, but I knew it was true.

I was coming up on a cross street when a man wearing a filthy suit stepped out from around the corner of the building ahead and directly into my path. Bent with age, he turned bleak red eyes to me and stared. Pressed to his chest with both hands he carried a paperback book as soiled and bereft as his suit. Are you one of the real ones or not? he demanded. And after a moment, when I failed to answer, he walked on, resuming his sotto voce conversation.

A chill passed through me. Somehow, indefinably, I felt, felt with the kind of baffled, tacit understanding we have in dreams, that I had just glimpsed one possible future self.

15.

As it turned out, I didn't have any trouble finding the guys in berets. I just had to open the door.

I'd stopped off at the Chinaman's on Washington to walk a shrimp po-boy and got back to the house just as the sky went black and a hard rain started down. I undressed and propped myself up in bed with the sandwich, a pint of vodka and the book Straughter had stuffed in my mailbox. Rain slammed down outside. I dripped lettuce and dressing on the covers, sipped vodka and read about Meursault. He has this nothing job and life, doesn't cry at his mother's funeral, later on kills an Arab because the sun's so bright, and he's writing all this down, or telling it, while awaiting his execution, but he still doesn't feel anything. I couldn't make a lot of sense out of it. So once the sandwich and most of the bottle were gone, so was I. I slid down into covers, turned off the light and was asleep before the afterimage on my retinas faded.

I got in two solid hours before someone started kicking my door.

Probably they weren't kicking the door, but that's how it sounded. I struggled to the surface and to my feet, stumbled downstairs to the door and opened it. Not mules at all. Two guys in black shirts and berets, one's skin as black as his shirt, the other's the color of *café au lait*. The rain had stopped. Light caught on water in trees, in pools on the ground.

"You Griffin?" the darker one said.

Apparently everyone in town knew where I lived.

"Why not. Sure." I left the door open, turned, and walked into the kitchen. "You guys want coffee or something? A beer, maybe."

There was coffee left over in the pot. I poured it in a saucepan and set it on a burner.

"We don't use stimulants," Au Lait said. He pushed the door shut behind him.

"Or abuse our bodies with alcohol," Blackie added.

"Okay. You ever use chairs?" I waved toward those around the table.

"We'll stand."

"Your call."

Steam rolled above the pan. I poured coffee into a mug, added milk. Blisters of fat formed on top. I sniffed the milk in the carton. Not bad. I'd drunk worse.

"So what can I do for you gentlemen? Since you didn't drop by for coffee or to use my chairs."

They looked at one another.

"Gentlemen," Blackie said.

The other cocked his head briefly to one side and back. Strange world out here.

"You've been asking about . . . an incident," Blackie said. "Took place at Dryades and Terpsichore?"

"Yeah?"

"Best stop asking," Au Lait told me.

"It's a local thing." Blackie. Conciliatory. "No one needs waves."

I sipped coffee.

"Sorry," I said. "Nigguh ain spose ta unnerstand all this, right? Jus spose ta do what chu say."

Blackie stared at me a moment. "It's complicated, Griffin."

"Sure is."

"Discretion's called for."

"I think I may still have a little bit of that tucked away at the back of my underwear drawer. Some I saved just in case. You want me to go look?"

I dumped the rest of the coffee in the sink and pulled a Jax out of the icebox.

"What do you know?" Blackie said.

A reasonable question.

I told him.

"Where do you think all that money came from, Lewis?"

"Contributions, I heard."

"Right. And Tar Baby came on strong in the primaries." He picked up my bottle and took a healthy swig, set it back down in the circle it came out of.

"Body handling the abuse okay?" I said.

"Yeah, they told us you're a smart mouth."

"And a tough guy."

I shrugged. "Hobbies."

"Say no one pushes you around, or stops you when you don't want to be stopped."

"I have breaks and bruises to prove it."

"You've also got about the strangest reputation I ever rubbed up against. I asked around. Three out of four people tell me you're crazy as batshit, the original bad news, cross the street. Then the fifth or sixth one I talk to says he'd trust you with his life."

"Kind of work I do, those two things aren't mutually exclusive."

Blackie nodded. "So I figure it like this: your own way, you're a soldier too."

"For about ten minutes—but I blinked."

"What?"

"They threw me out."

He smiled. There was no humor in the smile. "Exactly. They've thrown us all out. For three hundred years. Out of their buildings, their neighborhoods, their schools, their professions, their establishment, their society. That's what all this is about, right?"

For a time when I was a kid back in Arkansas, every Saturday night someone blackened the face of the Doughboy statue on Cherry Street with shoe polish. And each Sunday morning one of the jail trustees was out there scrubbing it clean. You see how it is, Lewis, my father said. We raise his children for him, cook for him, bring up his crops, butcher his hogs, even fight his wars for him, and he still won't acknowledge our existence, we're still invisible.

"Revolution," Au Lait said reverently.

"Lots of small revolutions," Blackie went on, "all taking place on their own. Local groups, communities, brotherhoods, churches. All over the country. People helping bring it along in their own way. People like us. Wave after wave coming together, growing."

"This guy that's been shooting people: he one of your waves? One of your revolutionaries?"

"Absolutely not. We abhor and decry violence in any form."

"Unusual attitude for a soldier."

"There's more than one kind of soldier, Griffin. Some only keep the peace."

Au Lait: "That's why we're here."

It was a thought I'd had before: few things are more frightening than a person who's rendered his life down to this single thing. Religion, sex or alcohol, politics, racism—it doesn't much matter what the thing is. You look into his eyes and see the covered light, sense something of the very worst we can come to, individually and collectively. But one of the things that's even scarier is people who haven't rendered their lives down to anything at all.

"Excuse me," I said. "I came in in the middle of this movie. I don't know the plot. Who the characters are. Why everyone's zipping around so purposefully onscreen."

Blackie thought it over. "Our intelligence people tell us that you were brought in on Yoruba's side."

"In which case your intelligence—with, believe me, no personal slur intended—is sadly lacking. So perhaps you'll at least raise the level of mine?"

"Then what's your interest in this?" Blackie said.

"I've already told you. The shooter."

"He has nothing to do with it."

"That's my point. But after two hours' sleep in, I don't know, three or four days, I've got a couple of guys in funny hats standing here in my kitchen either trying to serve me slices off tomorrow's pie-in-the-sky or threatening me. Hard to tell."

"You're not working for Yoruba?"

"I'm not working for anyone. I have a few dollars put away that just *might* get me through the next week or so, and not much prospect of any more coming in—with rent and groceries happening soon. But a friend of mine went down in front of me. That's not history or half-assed political doctrine, that's real. It's not going to go away. I won't let it."

Blackie didn't say anything for a while. Au Lait walked over to the window and stood looking out.

"Maybe I've misjudged you," Blackie said.

"It happens."

He held out his hand. "Leo Tate. That's Clifford."

Au Lait glanced back from the window and nodded.

"Good to meet you both," I said.

16.

As I look back now, the whole thing's like a cross-country bus ride, long stretches of inaction punctuated by brief release, the feverish bustle of stops.

There were the accommodations of early years when the walls first started giving way, when suddenly we were able to sit at lunch counters, to enter stores, theaters, rooms previously denied us—when we began to become visible. And when we were joyful at these changes.

I remember bathrooms marked *Colored* disappearing. I remember walking through front doors for the first time in my life.

We breathed the high, rich air of social challenge, justice, freedom, inalienable rights. But that road, we discovered, penetrated just so far into the wilderness. It ended abruptly, without fanfare or warning, pavement abutting implacable forest. Here ships fall off the edge of the world. Here there be tigers.

Then a great rage. Calls for revolution. Roving patrols of self-appointed guardians. Armies of liberation operating out of vans, storefronts, project tenements.

Later, depending who described it, an embracing of or assault on local politics. Councilmen in place, city and state representatives, a mayor or two. Increments of power.

And finally this unspoken apartheid we live with still.

While the rage turns back on itself. Gnaws away at individuals, families, communities, cities. Begins to consume them.

That evening Straughter came by and spirited me off to Dillard University where we stood close together among similar huddles of others sipping wine from plastic cups and choking down rubbery cheese cubes. An usher in a jacket shiny with wear pushed open double doors giving us access to the small auditorium. Within minutes the room filled to capacity. Latecomers stood shuffling feet, coats over arms, at the back of the hall.

A black man in his fifties, light-skinned, wearing the collegiate uniform of chinos, vest sweater, chambray shirt, tweed sportcoat, came onstage and spoke inaudibly into the microphone there on the podium. He looked off left, shook his head, tried again.

"... welcome you to the first in a series of programs of lectures, readings and performances celebrating African-American art.

"I'm John Dent, and I teach literature—*English*, we're taught to call it—here at Dillard. Over the years I've likely taught many of you here tonight in this room. I may have *tried* to teach others."

Polite laughter.

"Those of you who managed to stay awake while I talked about Claude McKay, Mark Twain, Zora Hurston, Richard Wright, Hemingway or Jimmy Baldwin no doubt will remember that I've a special place in my heart and mind for the man I'm about to introduce to you.

"And now I warn you: prepare yourselves.

"Chester Himes is angry. *Very* angry.

"Chester Himes has been angry for a long time. Those of us who bothered to listen began understanding just *how* angry he was, how damaged, with his first novels: *If He Hollers, Lonely Crusade, The Third Generation*.

"Then Himes, like many another before him, discouraged, despairing, fled these United States for residency abroad. He lives now, has lived for some time, in France. And from there he's sent back to us a stream of project reports, communicados, indictments: mirrors showing this country's true face.

"First there was *The Primitive*, dropped like a grenade into the maw of fifties placidity. Truly dangerous, and a novel to match America's scant handful of almost perfect novels."

Professor Dent cleared his throat. Swept his eyes over those gathered before him. This was something he knew how to do. He was good at it. There were not many things in life he'd been good at.

"When I was a child, growing up on the banks of the Mississippi, we would catch alligator gar, prop their mouths open with sticks and put them back in the water. They'd rise and dive, rise, dive, till finally they went down for good. Submarines, we called these drowning monsters.

"And that's *The Primitive*. Subversive, ferocious. Rising out of depths America has never imagined, never acknowledged, and sinking back into them. Teeth bared. Dying."

Another purposeful pause.

"More recently Himes has given us several short novels featuring Harlem detectives Gravedigger Jones and Coffin Ed Johnson. Originally written for French publisher Gallimard at Marcel Duhamel's instigation—written for quick money and quickly, unabashed potboilers in the tradition of Faulkner's *Sanctuary*, a novel which greatly influenced them—these books appear in the States in paperback only, from various publishers, and on racks in drugstores alongside such monuments of American culture as *I, The Jury, Housewife Hustlers* and the current month's new Perry Mason.

"In these books Chester Himes continues to document, as no one else has done, the range of the African-American struggle, from subjection and capitulation to challenge and change.

"I submit to you now that in writing these books—'telling it like it is,' our children would say—Chester Himes, again and again, has committed nothing less than. Acts. Of. Absolute. Heroism."

Stepping back from the podium, Dent began applauding. Applause caught here and there in the audience and spread.

The man who shambled onstage did not look heroic. More than anything else, he looked tired. He was tall, light on his feet and subtly elegant in the way that dancers often are, with delicate features, close-cropped hair, medium skin. He wore a black suit that fit well enough to have been tailored, navy-and-maroon tie, starched white shirt. When the applause died and he looked up, his eyes were dark, intense and full, glimmers of emotion and understanding spilling out from them even as they swept in the finest details of the physical world around them.

Vitriol? Impassioned speech? Anger?

You better believe it.

But at the same time a rare truth: this gentle, cultivated voice, at first so low we could barely hear it, urging us on toward what we *might be,* imploring us to settle for nothing less than the best within us. To recognize that we had been set against ourselves, turned into our own worst enemy. Whenever walls get torn down, he said, the bricks are simply carried off elsewhere, another wall put up.

He read briefly from *The Primitive* and *If He Hollers,* and concluded:

"If our plumbing for truth, whether as a writer, like myself, or simply as individuals looking back over our experiences—if this plumbing for truth reveals within the Negro personality homicidal mania, lust, a pathetic sense of inferiority, arrogance, hatred, fear and self-despite, we must recognize this as the effect of oppression on the human personality. For these are the daily horrors, the daily realities, the daily experiences—the life—of black men and women in America."

Too soon it was over.

Lights came back full. All around us people stood, retrieving coats, streaming into the aisle.

"You want to hit the reception?" Straughter said.

Why not.

So we ate more crackers and cheese cubes and drank more wine out of plastic cups.

At Dr. Dent's house, amidst clusters of academics, students and activists, Himes sat on the couch pouring Jack Daniels into his coffee mug. When the other person there left, I sat down beside him, and without saying anything he reached over and poured into my own cup.

"Not a writer are you?" he asked.

"No."

"Teacher?"

I shook my head.

"Good. You stay there."

And I did, bourbon periodically splashing into my cup, till three hours later I struggled to my feet, said good-bye to Himes, somehow found Straughter and the door and walked through the latter with the former.

That morning once Leo and Clifford left (well, really now it was the day before), I'd toppled back into bed and slept straight through, fourteen, fifteen hours, till Straughter came banging at the door to bear me off. Verne had been by and left another note that said "Even zombies get up and walk around sometimes, Lew.'' I think someone else pounded at the door at one point, but that may have been a part of the dream in which I found myself wandering in a foreign land where buildings, trees, the whole landscape were unrecognizable. Two groups lived there, neither of whose language I could understand at all, neither of which seemed much to care whether I stayed with them or straggled off again to the other. Mostly they spent their time gouging and pounding wood into canoelike boats they never used.

Straughter and I were both pretty drunk, and after an hour or so of stumbling around saying things like "We already *been* by here" and "House looks awful familiar," we finally admitted that we had no idea where he'd parked his Falcon—or for that matter, after all this, where *we* were.

Probably just as well, Straughter said, he ought not be trying to drive anyway. So what the hell, he'd just hoof it on home. Could almost always do that in N'Orleans. Come back later today and hunt down the Blue Bird. Wouldn't be the first time.

"Need to head over that way," he said, absolutely certain of it. "Yep. To-ward Freret," the preposition two syllables.

"River's *that* way, Hosie."

But he was adamant, mule stubborn as my folks used to say, so we parted.

I walked toward the river until (I was right!) I hit St. Charles. Then down it toward town. The streetcar had long since stopped running. There was little traffic.

At some point, I remember, for whatever reason, taking off my shoes. Striding along barefoot, oblivious to how broken and uneven the sidewalks were.

I remember stepping off at last into cool, damp grass for relief.

I remember dogs barking and leaping at fences just inches from me.

I remember a police car cruising slowly by me, once, twice, as I trod along, pacing me, pausing a third time alongside with the crackle of its radio audible, at last passing on.

Fragments.

I awoke that afternoon with feet so bloody and torn that I could barely hobble to the bathroom, to a tub of warm water with baking soda. Three beers lined up tubside to help quell pounding heart and head, nausea, shakes.

Not only had I taken to hot pavement in bare feet, I had first hiked to my old apartment on Dryades. When the key failed to work, I realized my lapse and walked back up to Washington. Though not by any direct route, I'm afraid: I had vague memories of far-flung parts of the city.

In the tub I swallowed beer the way a beached fish gasps at air and thought over what Leo and Clifford had told me yesterday morning.

Yoruba was an inkblot, they said: many things to many people. For some it *was* basically religious, a church. Others perceived it as essentially activist, which, certain ways, certain times, it was; and that was what attracted *them*. Some were drawn to, saw as foremost, its community service.

"I see what you mean. All things to all men."

Leo nodded.

"Tough part for any actor."

"You have a lot of eggs, they won't fit in a single basket," Leo said. "You take care of them."

"You're saying Yoruba's not straight? That the game's fixed?"

"I'm saying the house always has the odds."

Clifford spoke up: "There's another thing. Another side of Yoruba, another service it provides."

"Banking," Leo said.

"A lot of people in the community resent white banks. Don't trust them—or just don't want to have to deal with them. Yoruba's their bank."

17.

"He's become invisible," Walsh said. "Gone to ground."

Or more likely to air, I thought: up.

"I do keep running into your friend Doo-Wop. Ask me, I think he likes the idea of working with a cop."

"He have anything?"

Walsh shook his head.

"Sooner or later, he will. Of course, it could just as easily be three years from now as it could be next week."

"And he wouldn't recognize the difference."

"Exactly."

Four P.M. We were sitting in Dunbar's, at a table whose top still showed evidence of the noontime rush: crumbs, splotches of sauce, a plug of bread lodged against the sugar bowl. Several tables remained uncleared. Officially the restaurant was closed, and we were the only customers. The owners—Alphée Dunbar, whom everyone called Tia, her companion of fifty-some years, Gilbert, and a somewhat younger man, John Gaunt, whose role both in restaurant and the others' private life had been all these years a matter of speculation—sat at the table nearest the kitchen over a steaming pot of barbequed shrimp. A platter of ribs covered most of our own table. We each had a couple of beers lined up there too. On the TV up by the cash register Danny Thomas had just given way to Science Fiction Theater. The sound was turned off.

I filled Walsh in on my visit from beret brothers Leo and Clifford, what they'd had to say about Yoruba. He told me yeah, NOPD'd been running into these rumors about some kind of underground banking organization for two, three years now. Word was, it just might violate a handful of federal laws, in principle if not letter, and both the FBI and T-men were supposed to be looking into it.

The police didn't think either the FBI *or* Treasury Agents could find their own asses, mind you.

Walsh dropped a slab of rib back on the platter. It looked like piranha had stripped it clean to the bone. He pulled a paper napkin off the stack of them delivered with the ribs and wiped mouth, chin, fingers.

"These guys in the hats," he said. "They potential heroes? Kind that might take things into their own hands?"

"I don't get that feeling, no."

"Good. Enough vigilantes running around already. So how far *are* these guys bent?"

"Hard to say. The gleam's there in their eyes, no doubt about that. But you can still see around it. So can they."

"For now, anyway." Walsh killed his first beer and put the bottle down. It was smeared with barbeque sauce. "Dangerous?"

"I don't think so. Could be to themselves, given the right circumstances."

"Or the wrong ones."

I nodded.

Then we both concentrated on our ribs and no one said anything more for a while. Just lots of animal noises, as LaVerne would put it.

John Gaunt went behind the counter for another beer and glanced over to see if perhaps we might be in need as well. Walsh stuck up a couple of fingers. What the hell. He had three days off. And I'd had a rough week. Not to mention feet resembling hamburger.

"Still no connection between these guys and the shooter, way you see it? Or this Yoruba thing?"

"Other than the fact there's no one here but us chickens, you mean. Not that I can make out."

"So why hasn't he stepped forward again? Man seemed awful damn determined. You know? But it's been a long time now since the last killing."

"Could be his knowing you're back here behind him has a lot to do with it. Having to watch over his shoulder."

I set my empty bottle alongside his. John Gaunt thumped new ones, held between first and second fingers, onto the table and snagged the empties between third and fourth fingers, all in a single sweep.

"This isn't some repressed accountant or crazed cabdriver who one night watched a TV show that shook him loose from his moorings then grabbed his old man's gun from the closet and headed off to restore justice to the world. This guy's no wig-out. Not a Quixote, either.

"Or maybe," I said, "come to think of it, he is. But whatever else he is, the man's a soldier.

"Think about it. He's behind enemy lines. Hell, he *lives* in enemy territory. There's nothing he can take for granted—nothing. Nothing's safe. He can't trust the people he comes across. Can't trust the language, can't trust the water, can't even trust whatever new orders might reach him. Now someone, another soldier, is crowding up close behind him. The enemy knows he's here. The enemy's seen him. What else can he do—"

"—but become invisible?"

"Exactly."

"And wait."

"Exactly."

But we didn't wait long.

"Regardez," Alphée said.

John Gaunt walked over to turn up the TV's sound. Our eyes went with him.

A street scene. Block-long stretch of low Creole cottages fanning out behind, downtown New Orleans looming in the distance, lots of open sky. Reporter in tailored suit and silk blouse holding mike. Full lips, good teeth, golden eyes. Sound of traffic close by.

Just moments ago, in what was believed may have been the latest in a series of terrorist-style killings, a resident in cardiology at Charity Hospital was gunned down in the parking lot of this convenience store near the river.

The camera pulls away to show a stretcher being fed into an ambulance. All around the ambulance are police cars with headlights aglare, bubblelights sweeping.

Coming off forty-eight straight hours on call, much of it spent at the front lines of a battlefield most of us couldn't even imagine—

gunshot wounds, knifings, drug overdoses, a man who fell asleep on the tracks and was run over by a train—Dr. Lalee had told co-workers she planned to stop off for coffee, half 'n' half and frozen pizza on the way home, then spend the next two days in bed with several good books of resolutely nonmedical sort.

A single bullet—fired, officials believed, from an abandoned factory nearby—ended those plans. Ended *all* this physician's plans. And ended, as well, a young woman's life. A fine young woman who against her parents' wishes relocated here from Palestine. Who had chosen New Orleans as the place where she would serve her final years of medical apprenticeship. Where she would become a part of the team working to provide our community a level of medical care elsewhere unsurpassed.

Now, even as we watch from our living rooms, other members of that team worked frantically to save Dr. Lalee's life. One of their own.

This, just in from Charity Hospital.

The camera pulls back to the announcer's face.

Chief of staff Dr. Morris Petrovich has announced that, at 4:56 local time, despite heroic measures on the part of physicians and staff, Dr. Lalee, a resident in their own cardiology section, expired of complications accruing from a gunshot to the chest.

18.

Someone once said life is all conjunctions, just one damn thing after another. But so much of it's not connected. You're sliding along, hit a bump and come down in a life you don't recognize. Every day you head out a dozen different directions, become a dozen different people; some of them make it back home that night, others don't.

When I came home from Dunbar's, just after dark, Verne was there waiting.

Walsh and I had driven by the CircleCtop on Tchoupitoulas. The block was still choked with emergency vehicles and gawkers. Walsh decided to head back downtown, dropped me off on the way.

Happy hunting, I told him.

Verne sat in the front room in her slip with the lights off. Her dress was draped over the back of an easy chair. She'd poured a couple fingers of Scotch into a glass and sipped her way down to the first finger.

"Walking like an old man there, Lewis."

I told her why.

"Not infected, are they?" She got up and walked toward me. "You really do need to start taking better care of yourself, have I mentioned that?" She reached up and put her arms around me. "Good to see you anyhow. Old, infected, whatever."

"You do know how to flatter a man, Miss LaVerne."

I always felt like I'd hit one of those bumps with LaVerne. Like I'd hit a *lot* of those bumps.

"I put some coffee on," she said. "Or maybe you want a drink instead. Have you eaten?"

I didn't say anything, just held on to her.

"I miss you so much when you're away, Lew. Or when I am."

I nuzzled her neck, kissed one bare shoulder.

"I always tell myself: this time he won't be back. That's the kind of thing women think, the kind of fears we live with. But it's never that I'm afraid you've found someone else, stopped caring about me, wanting to be with me. What I'm afraid of, is that you're dead somewhere."

"Someday I will be."

"And how long will it be before I even know it? How will I find out? I'll just think you're away again. Working. Business as usual.

"Women wait. That's what we do, what we learn, what we become. No one else ever knows how much waiting can hurt."

She climbed out of bed to grab a couple of beers.

"You matter to me, Lew," she said, handing over a bottle. "That's the thing."

"I know."

So I held her to keep her from the foggy, foggy dew.

Porgy you is my man.

Later she lit a cigarette and lay beside me smoking. This small red beacon there in the darkness. I listened to her breath go in, hold, come back out. Felt the bed move with it, move again with her arm.

"Lew. I never told you about my folks, did I?"

"Unh-unh," I said, near sleep.

"I will some time."

"Ummmm."

She took a final draw and stubbed the cigarette out.

"Welcome home, Lew," she said. Then: "Home is the sailor, home from the sea. And the hunter, home from the hill."

"Hmmmm?"

"Nothing. You go on to sleep, honey. I'll lie here a while with you."

Later still, I felt her swing her legs slowly out of bed so as not to disturb me, heard the whisper of her dress sliding over the nylon slip. The bathroom door closed. The light came on. Water ran into the sink. The light went off. Cat-soft footsteps from bathroom to front door. Door eased shut around the latch's fall.

For the first time it came to me that we're damned every bit as much by the things we don't do as by things we do.

When she was gone I snapped on the light and read *The Stranger* from cover to cover.

19.

I finally got to sleep at two in the morning and dreamed I was walking along a beach in Algiers—the real one, not the one across the river. People all around me were frozen in position, lifting carafes of water, turning pages, gesturing to those beside them, running out toward the water. Then I was in a white room with no furniture and with paintings, also white, in white frames, on the walls. Everything outside the windows was white too, and you couldn't tell windows from paintings from walls. My patron asked if I would like to go to work in the home office. Suddenly then, I was there: in Paris. But it looked more like New Orleans, like the Quarter that grew out of the great fire of the 1850's. I lay prone on a rooftop. A hot sun hung just above; sweat ran on the back of my neck, soaked my shirt. Below, an Arab stepped through the corner doorway of the Napoleon House. I felt my finger begin to tighten on the trigger. His face turned abruptly up to me. It was the shooter. He smiled and threw out his arms.

I awoke to avoid the bullet's impact as it hurtled toward me. Tried for a moment to make some sense of tatters of the dream spinning away, dissolving. Impossible to guess what time it was. And the clock had long since run down. Wallowing on my stomach like an alligator to bed's edge and over, I turned on the radio.

A play, set on Lepers' Island. Young Marcel, having inadvertently killed the woman he loves, has come here to reassert his humanity, to redeem himself in voluntary service. All is in chaos. No fellowship, no society, remains here. It's every man for himself. And though he has first to learn the language even to get by, slowly Marcel contrives to bring inhabitants together. He helps them reestablish basic social structures and services, leads them to acknowledge once again their need for individual and collective responsibility—to the point, in fact, that he realizes his work here is done. Only when the next supply ship puts into port, the one he believed would bear him back to his old world, does Marcel learn that he has become a leper himself.

"I saw it in the eyes of the crewmen," he says at the end, music welling up beneath, "the fear, the aversion: what I had become. How could I not have known? Except, of course, that I had sunk so completely into this community, reinventing myself within it, that I was no longer able to perceive myself outside its standards."

Dramatic music spilled up and over, sponsors and production members were thanked. Then a station I.D. Finally, the time: 5:40. I'd been asleep just a little over three hours.

I rolled left, right, onto my back, onto my stomach, almost onto the floor—and gave up. By then it was 6:21. Evidently the swan of sleep wasn't coming back for me, however eagerly I awaited it. And outside, the city was stirring in its bed, stretching, throwing off covers, clearing its vast throat.

I filled a saucepan with water. When it was boiling I tossed in a handful of coffee. Let it steep and settle a few minutes, dumped it into a mug half full of milk. Perfect.

I crawled back in bed and picked up *The Stranger* again. Got up twice and made coffee. Got up about page 150 and poured a glass of Scotch.

Got up halfway through the Scotch to answer the door.

Those PI's in the novels have it all wrong. You don't have to go out and track people down. You just wait around the house and sooner or later the people come and find *you*. It had worked with Leo and Clifford. Now it was working again. Maybe I was on to something.

"You're Griffin." He looked as though he wouldn't be surprised if I felt a need to apologize for it.

I didn't, so I just stood there looking at him.

He stood there looking back at me.

Fine way to pass the morning. We were two damn tough brothers, better believe it. Seasons could change around us, leaves falling from the trees, baby ducks swimming in the pond, we'd still be standing there.

What the hell. Even the Buckingham guards change shift and go home.

"Why don't we glare at one another inside? That okay with you?"

I turned and walked out to the kitchen. He came along, four paces behind.

"You want anything? Carrot juice, distilled water?"

"Beer'd be nice, if you have one. Or whatever *you* happen to be drinking."

I'd brought my glass with me when I answered the door.

"Scotch okay? Johnny Walker?"

"Doesn't get any more okay than that."

I found another glass for him, poured in some amber, freshened my own.

I sat at the kitchen table. Maybe since he drank he'd want to use my chairs too.

Yep.

So we sat there a bit, sipping at one another now instead of glaring.

"Usually, people come by to have a drink with me," I said, "they want to talk a little while they're here."

He took another taste, ran it around his tongue.

"Of course, it's not *required* ..."

He swallowed. "Saw you at that Himes thing the other night. You ever read his stuff?"

I shook my head.

"Me either. But I've sure *heard* a lot about it."

Some silent bell rang then, and we went to our separate corners. No one said anything. I leaned the chair back, reached and got the bottle off the counter and set it on the table between us. He waited for me to offer and pour. Then he moved as though to hunch down over the glass with both hands wrapped around it—just for a second before he cut it off, but I caught the glimpse.

"You've done time," I said.

He sipped, swallowed. Pulled his lips back tight against his teeth. "What makes you say that?"

"You mean aside from the fact you're black and well into your twenties? Given that, and the city, what are the odds you *haven't*?

But what I pick up on is this special kind of courtesy you show—a respect. You didn't even look at the bottle when I put it down: it was mine, I'd have to make the move. Then when I poured you a drink, for just a minute you started to hunch down over it. Like you used to hunch over food in the cafeteria. Or hootch back in the cell. It gets to be instinctive.''

"You been there too, else you wouldn't know that.''

"I didn't do any serious time. Enough to see what it was like.''

He nodded. "Yeah, you're right. I did two pulls. Been a while now. Ten-to-fifteen on grand theft auto, another nickel on armed robbery. That's where I first started hearing about Himes. He was big on the yard. Almost like he was right there with us sometimes. He wasn't, of course. He was off in Paris living in some rich man's house drinking wine with every meal. Brothers never wanted to hear that. And that's a whole other thing. But what he wrote, what he said: he got it right.''

I poured some more into our glasses.

"You get much sleep?'' I asked.

"What you want to know that for?''

"Just wondering. Kind of an informal poll. I don't seem to be able to snag much of it lately. Sleep, I mean. Makes me wonder whether someone else isn't getting my share.''

He looked at me. "Damn, Griffin. You may just be as strange as people say you are. Doo-Wop said when I found you you'd likely as not be spouting something you found in some book nobody else'd ever read.''

Doo-Wop was telling people *I* was strange? First chance that came along, I'd have to sit down and think about that.

"Doo-Wop sent you?''

"Well, yeah. Kind of.''

"And he told you where to come? Knew where I lived?''

He nodded.

Of course Doo-Wop knew. He didn't know what day or year it was, but he knew where I lived. Everyone knew. Pretty soon lost kids were going to start showing up at the door. Tourists from New Jersey out to see the real New Orleans.

Time to find new quarters, Lewis.

"I, uh . . .'' my guest went on. "This is just between the two of us, right?''

Right.

"I have a regular job, you understand. French-bread bakery out on Airline. Been there five, six years. Take care of my family. But time to time I still play a chorus or two off the old song, you know? Friend from those days comes to you, bills gobble up the paycheck by the fifteenth, baby needs new shoes. You know?"

I knew.

"Figured you did."

I hit us again with the Scotch. He nodded, acknowledgment and thanks. Took the obligatory ceremonial sip.

"Things go well, after a job the players want to step out, unwind some, have a drink or two. Long about the third drink sometimes they'll get to talking. Just like at the bakery on breaks. Same thing."

"Yeah."

"One of those nights this guy Julio and I had hit it off good, and after the others went on home, we stayed there, place called El Gore-e-adore or something, drinking. Develops that Julio's a real pro, this is all he does. Pulls a spot as wheelman one day, does a little strong-arm turn the next, maybe goes in as backup on a heavy job.

"By this time it's, I don't know, two, three in the morning, and Julio tells me this story that's about all I remember the next day when I wake up.

"Couple days after that, I'm lifting a few with the Doo Man. You know how that man likes a good story. So pretty soon I get to feeling good, way one does, and I tell him the whole thing, what Julio told me. When I'm through he just nods. Then after a while he says, Good story. After a little more, he tells me: Needs footnotes, though. I just look at him. Have to identify your sources, he says. And I think: This man's been hanging around those uptown college campuses too much.

"Anyhow, he says I've got to come see you."

"And he tells you where I live."

"Even buys me a drink. Paying for the story—you know?"

Oh yes. "And?"

"Well, it's not much. Only worth one drink to the Doo Man, mind you."

"This a commercial transaction?"

"No no. Not what I mean at all. I don't want you to think this is some big thing. It's just warm air, a breeze, cotton. I'm only here—

wasting time I could put to better use—because Doo-Wop says you're all right. Friend of a friend kind of thing, you know?"

"Meanwhile having a few friend of a friend kind of drinks."

He nodded. "A few."

"Maybe a few more?"

"Whatever the market will bear."

I poured. He nodded. We sipped.

"There's this hardass Julio worked with a couple times. Guess they went out unwinding after some turns too. Man's day job is with a security service. SeCure Corps. Black-owned and -operated. I've seen their advertisements. They're all standing on the steps of some building in tight suits and bowties. Look like a bunch of CPA's.

"And they're all avowed nonviolents. So from time to time on this or that job—just to protect themselves—they bring in backup."

"Bodyguards."

"More like contract soldiers. World's changing, you know? Whatever your beliefs, you either change with it or you go under. Disappear like the dinosaurs.

"Anyway. One of the people they use most often, a marksman, calls himself The Sentry. That's how they get in touch with him— run a personal ad for 'The Sentry' in *The Griot*. No one ever sees him. He responds with a similar ad of his own. Day before, he calls in from a pay phone for details. D-day, he signals his presence and position with a mirror flash."

"A sniper."

"You got it."

"He ever had to shoot?"

"Not yet."

"Good luck."

He nodded.

"How does he get paid, once it's over?"

"Post office box. Yeah: it changes every time. And the one time SeCure Corps staked it out, some kid on a bicycle came pedaling up to collect. They didn't hear from The Sentry for a while after that. When they did, he wondered if SeCure Corps truly valued and required his services."

"And?"

"They backed off."

"So this is a long-term association."

"It's got history, yeah."

"Pay well?"

"Expect so. From all I hear, these guys are going flat out, full throttle."

"You have to wonder just where the support's coming from."

"Few others wondering about that right along with you."

20.

"Yes, sir, how may I help you?"

"Personnel, please."

"May I ask in regard to what?"

"I'm calling to inquire about employment with your firm."

"Then it's Mr. Bergeron you'd be needing. Please hold. I'll see if Mr. Bergeron's in his office."

He was, but it took us both a while to find out.

I was calling from a pay phone facing a Frostop on St. Charles. Icy mugs of root beer and some of the best hamburgers in town inside. One of your more fascinating processions outside.

A white guy minced past in denim miniskirt and pink tights through which you could see whorls of leg hair. Baby-blue sleeveless blouse above, breasts like those castanet-size finger cymbals Indian dancers use. His Adam's apple stuck out a lot further. He kept brushing at the blond wig and catching himself just before he fell off three-inch heels. Arms suddenly out at his sides like a tightrope walker's.

A young woman in high-collared white blouse, oversize spectacles, and a dress that swept fastfood wrappers from the sidewalk as she passed. Walking beside a pure Marlon Brando type in T-shirt, jeans, and scowl, a foot shorter than she was.

Unshaven older guy in a baseball cap with belly arranged just so over the Texas-shaped buckle of his belt, belly and torso encased like sausage in a black T-shirt reading *Love a Trucker—Or Do Without*.

"Hello? Are you still there? Please hold, I'm trying to track down Mr. Bergeron."

At least she didn't switch me over to Hawaiian music or an arrangement of "Mack the Knife" for strings. Just a dead line with ghost voices far back, unintelligible, within it.

A thirtyish woman with bleach-blonde hair, bright red lipstick, tight cashmere sweater and full skirt came by. The Marilyn Monroe look, I suppose.

When he came on, he was breathing hard. Maybe he spent every lunch hour working out. Maybe when the receptionist tracked him down he took a shot at her. Or maybe he was just fat off other people's work. The world was what you made it. Sure it was.

"Bergeron here. Please. To whom am I speaking?"

I told him.

"And you're interested in employment, my secretary says. In what capacity, if I might ask?"

I sketched my background in paper serving, skip tracing, bodyguard and security work. Most of the last was pure invention, but set up by the rest, which *was* true, it sounded good.

"Well," he said. "Ordinarily we wouldn't consider accepting an application over the phone. I'm sure you understand. But as it turns out, we find ourselves in need of extra help tonight—unexpectedly. A good and regular customer. Else we would have declined. And you do seem to be the kind of experienced professional we're always looking for."

"Had a feeling this might turn out to be a good day," I said.

"First name spelled L-O-U-I-S?"

I corrected him, then went ahead and spelled my last name too.

"And you're currently employed . . . ?"

"I'm not—though not for lack of trying, I assure you. Generally I work freelance. Bodyguard work, collections, like I told you. And I walk a lot of paper for Boudleaux & Associates. But things have been getting thin for a while now."

"Frankie DeNoux?"

"Yeah."

"I know him. Everybody knows him."

"Seems like it."

"Your training?"

"Military."

No reason to tell him I'd gone from civilian to MP back to civilian in a hop and a skip. More skip than hop, come to think of it.

"Address?"

"Wouldn't do you much good. I move around a lot." I had my fish, I could slack off now.

"I understand. Some place you can be reached, then? Since the law requires it."

I gave him Verne's address.

"Social Security number?"

"Let's see . . ." I tried a couple of three-digit sequences. "Sorry. Can't remember it just this minute."

"No problem. Happens all the time. Just bring it in when you come by for your check."

"Then I have work?"

"Are you free from seven to around twelve tonight?"

"I can be."

"Then you have work. Pays four dollars an hour, four hours guaranteed, probably run between five and six. You'll need to be at Esplanade and Broad by seven at the latest. Report to Sam Brown. Big guy, hair and beard completely white. You can't miss him. He's front man on this, and whatever he says, goes. Checks will be ready to pick up here by four tomorrow afternoon. We can cash your check on the premises, if you want. Sam likes you, puts in a good word, we'll be using you again.

"Thank you for getting in touch with us, Mr. Griffin. Any questions?"

"Only one. What am I going to be doing?"

"Of course. I did fail to mention that, didn't I. You'll be working crowd control."

21.

"Gentlemen," Sam Brown said.

Bergeron was right, he looked like a fullback. Hell, he looked like two fullbacks. You could land fighter planes on his shoulders. He wore a black suit skillfully tailored to downplay his size, but man's ingenuity only goes so far.

"Most of you here, I've worked with you before. And *work*, for those new to SeCure Corps, is most definitely the operative word. We pay good money, we expect good value. You take care of business, we'll take care of you.

"Tonight's business is crowd control, people. You are intelligence, and intelligence only. You'll be teamed in pairs, given walkie-talkies and specific watches. You'll report in each fifteen minutes. You do not, repeat *not*, take any action. See anything unusual, anything suspicious, any sign of trouble, you get away from there and report back to me. And that's *all* you do. Is that understood?

"Officially the city anticipates that about three hundred people will show up tonight; they're prepared to handle twice that. Police estimates are running higher, maybe as many as a thousand, they say, before it's over, and the department has placed officers accordingly.

"The affair's sponsors, however, have reason to believe attendance may be well in advance of expectations. And you, gentlemen, we, are their insurance.

"I repeat: intelligence only. Circulate, observe, reconnoiter, report. Police officers both in uniform and plainclothes will be on watch for legal violations or for any possibility of violence. Federal agents are also present. We are here expressly as their helpmates, an early warning system. And the lower profile we keep, the more effective we can be."

Walking up Broad on my way here, I'd seen stragglers as far back as Canal, then as I approached Esplanade, more and more, until they were everywhere: stapled to telephone poles, abandoned storefronts and boarded-up houses, impaled on ironwork fences, stuck beneath the wipers of cars sitting on bare wheels at curbside.

> CORENE DAVIS
> TONIGHT!
> COMMUNITY HALL OF
> REDEEMER BAPTIST CHURCH
> 8 P.M.
> HEAR THE TRUTH

"Who's Corene Davis?" I asked the guy I got paired with. He was as thin as Sam Brown was broad. He could lie down, you'd think he was the horizon.

He shrugged with shoulders a sparrow would fall off. "Big shot in Black Rights, I guess. From up North somewhere. Man said your name was Louis?"

"Lew."

"James. You worked this before?"

"Not for SeCure Corps. Usually work on my own—freelance."

"Oh yeah? You ever need help?"

"Only finding customers."

"I know what that's like. Used to do sales, myself. Fine men's clothing. Only trouble was, no fine men ever came in to buy it, and I was on straight commission."

"What about you?"

"What about me."

I gestured around us.

"Oh. Yeah, I score a job with them a couple, three times a month. SeCure's good people. Pay a decent wage, never try to hold back on you. I've been trying to get on as a regular, but it's a long list."

The community center had already filled. Earlier in the day speakers had been set up outside, and now a huge crowd was forming, spilling off the sidewalk into the street and sidewalk opposite. It looked like Carnival had touched down. Most had brought food: bags of fried chicken, picnic baskets and cardboard boxes, coolers, po-boys in white butcher paper.

"Brown did say federal agents, am I right?"

We had our backs to the wall across the street, keeping watch on new arrivals.

"Word is," James said, "there've been threats."

"What kind of threats?"

"The death kind."

"Against Corene Davis."

He nodded. "They've kept it quiet. One of the regulars I worked with before told me."

"Who made the threats? How were they made?"

"That's been kept even quieter. Someone said by letter—white ink on black paper. I don't know. Yoruba's been mentioned. So has the group that wears purple shirts and berets. The Black Hand seems to be a current favorite."

Around the corner to our right came a group of young men, sixteen of them marching in formation, four-by-four. They wore black jeans and shirts and their heads were shaved. The leader, front left, called out the rhythm as they advanced. They executed the turn in finest drill form, at crowd's edge made a perfectly coordinated right-face and marked time as the leader counted down cadence. Then they stood erect and still, feet slightly apart, hands clasped in the small of their back, eyes forward.

"Don't you just love watching the little childrens play soldier?" a voice said to my left. As I turned that way, Leo Tate stepped up grinning, Clifford close behind.

"Yeah, get themselves some cool hats like yours, they'd really look sharp."

"Such a romantic soul, Lewis."

"I try. Had no idea you guys were interested in Corene Davis, though."

"We're interested in anyone who tries to tell the truth about being black in this country."

"You happen to know anything about threats against her life?"

The two of them exchanged glances. Clifford shrugged, shoulders moving maybe a quarter-inch. Leo nodded back in kind.

"We heard that, yeah. Mostly why we're here."

"Any idea who could be behind it?"

"You want the long list or the short one? Short one's almost as long as the long one—know what I'm saying?"

"Of course, there may be nothing to it all," Clifford said.

Static crackled on the walkie-talkie, and Leo looked down at my hand.

"Man, *everybody's* playing soldier today. They give you your official decoder badge too?"

"Friends of yours, I take it," James said after they had stepped off into the ever-thickening crowd. I looked at him. He just shook his head. "Takes all kinds."

I looked around us again. "Which is about what we've got here."

"For sure."

We made our way along the rear of the crowd, which by now had expanded well into the next block. People still streamed in from every direction. James called to report, cupping his hand over the walkie-talkie and all but shouting to be heard against the din.

We had turned to start back across when a hand fell on my shoulder and someone spoke behind me.

"Lewis. I can't help but notice that you seem to be taking a sudden, decided interest in black affairs these days."

"Working," I said. I held up the walkie-talkie.

Hosie looked at it, back at me. "That may be even more intriguing."

"Leaping to conclusions again?"

"Peering cautiously over the edge of one, anyhow. Go on about your business, Lewis, whatever it is. We can talk later."

We started across to check out the other side, noting that a half-dozen hardcases had grouped around the men in black with shaved heads. The hardcases were tossing insults and taunts at them. The sixteen men stood in formation looking straight ahead, making no response.

I glanced at James. He nodded and bent his head close to the walkie-talkie to call it in.

Cackles shot from the speakers outside the hall, then a loud, shrill peal before they were again shut down. After a moment a steady sizzling sound came back on. Several taps—of fingers? A clearing throat.

"Ladies . . . and . . . gentlemen.

"Brothers.

"Sisters.

"It is a great honor tonight to be called upon to introduce the young lady sitting here beside me. Rarely has the voice of our black nation, rarer still that of its youth, been heard so clearly, with such honesty and . . ."

Static obliterated the voice. There were further thumps. A murmur started through the crowd.

Momentarily the voice resurfaced: ". . . testimony to an enduring people." Then more static and, after a bit, speakers chopping his words into hiccups: "Ladies and gentlemen, please bear with us."

Static.

The crowd's murmur grew both in pitch and intensity.

". . . a minor technical problem, I'm told, now resolved. And so, with no more preamble or presumption, I present to you: Miss Corene Davis."

But apparently the technical problem wasn't that minor after all. Even as he spoke, speakers were cutting in and out, swallowing words and syllables.

"I would like to begin tonight," Corene Davis said once the applause had died down, "by quoting André Breton:

" 'Beauty,' he said, 'will be convulsive, or it will not exist.' "

It was then that the speakers cut out once and for all.

The crowd's murmur built to a roar. I could hear, from every corner, shouts and curses, raised voices, breaking glass. Fists went into the air. Tidelike surges shuddered through the mass of bodies around me. I watched as the sixteen men with shaved heads, as though on order, broke rank all at once and tore into the hardcases who had been heckling them.

Ten minutes later, we had a full-scale riot on our hands.

22.

"You do have a way of always being there, looking up just as the pigeons fly over."

"It's a gift."

"What the hell *were* you doing there?"

I told him.

"And you think there's a connection between the shooter and SeCure Corps?"

"This so-called Sentry's the only other person I've come across lately who's as shy as our sniper."

"Shy—and high."

"Exactly. Well worth checking out even if it weren't the only lead we had."

"Mr. Griffin?"

We both turned. A low-browed, acned young man in a lab coat stepped through the curtain. He was tall and gangly and looked to be all of sixteen, as though he ought to be mowing lawns and sitting at the movie wondering how to get an arm casually around his date's shoulder. Instead, here he was patching people back together and trying to save the occasional life.

"Your X-rays came back. Skulls series and cervical spine are okay, no problems there. That hand looks okay, as far as we can tell. No evidence of fracture. You're going to have one mother of a bruise, and the hand may swell up till you look like Mickey Mouse. However . . ."

The great medical however.

"... you have three cracked ribs. I don't think there's any danger, but we'd like you to stay here overnight for observation."

I shook my head. "Tape them."

"Mr. Griffin—"

I stopped him. "Doctor. I appreciate your concern, believe me. But I've been through this before."

"You don't understand. With injuries of this kind there's always the possibility of—"

"Lung puncture, pneumothorax, atalectasis, pneumonia. I *do* understand. As I said, this isn't exactly new territory for me. First time, I went to bed the way I was told and I got so sore it took me two months to get over it all. Next time, because someone was stalking me, I didn't have a choice, I had to keep moving. By the end of the week I'd almost forgotten it ever happened."

"Well ... you have a point. All right, Mr. Griffin. We'll do it your way, on a couple of conditions. One: you let me write a prescription for you in case the pain gets too bad, so you'll at least be able to rest."

"Second?"

"You come back day after tomorrow and let me take a look at you."

"Agreed." Though I knew there was little chance I'd come back. He probably knew it too.

"I'm still not clear on this thing with Davis," Walsh said as the doctor began wrapping me.

I looked beneath one raised arm.

"When all hell started breaking loose, I had to wonder if it might be a set-up. If the whole thing, the speaker trouble, the ensuing riot, all of it, hadn't started out just as a way to provide distraction."

"Making it easy for anyone who wanted to take Corene Davis down."

I nodded. "Hold still, Mr. Griffin," the doctor said.

"There wasn't anything I could do out on the edge like that. Man could have been standing in moonlight on the roof with a cannon and I wouldn't have seen him. So I pushed into the crowd. Thinking all the time that if I got in closer to the center, there was at least a chance I'd see something—assuming there was something to see.

"About this time they brought Corene Davis out a side door,

trying to get her away from danger. They came out of the church itself, not the community center, and I just happened to be in the right position and looking that way. Four men pressed close to her, and they were making for a black Lincoln parked in the alley behind.

"I caught a glimpse, just a flash of motion, from a doorway back there. I wasn't even sure, afterward, that I really saw it. But I went over the low stone wall between the buildings and along it, crouched as low as I could and still keep my speed up, and just as they reached the car, Corene and her escorts, this guy stepped out of the doorway."

"You broke his arm in two places, Lew. Witnesses said it looked like you were trying to tear it off. Then you started in on the rest of him."

"I don't know. I was concentrating on the gun. Funny how fast it came swiveling away from the others and toward me. All I wanted to do once he was down was make sure he *stayed* down. Man had one hell of a kick to him."

"Well, you took him down, all right. Hard. Be a while before he gets back up."

"Who is he?"

"We don't have much yet. His name's Titus Kyle, appears to be local. We've got his picture and prints on the wire, and feds are running a check for affiliations with subversive organizations, known activist groups and the like."

"He's an old man."

Walsh nodded. "Late fifties, anyway."

"Not the shooter."

"Nope."

"How does that feel, Mr. Griffin?" the doctor said.

I lowered my arms, twisted about, took a deep breath.

"Like someone's sitting on me."

"Perfect." He may even have smiled. "See you day after tomorrow." He scribbled on a pad, tore off the sheet and gave it to me. "Every four hours if you need it."

Walsh handed me my shirt. I managed to get it on without gasping.

"There's a line forming outside the ER door, you know. People taking numbers. Your dance card's filled. Five or six reporters, someone from the mayor's office. Man from SeCure Corps wants to offer you a full-time position. And Miss Davis is waiting to thank you personally."

I tucked the shirt in, put on my coat. "There a back way out of here?"

"That's what I thought you'd say. Yeah, there is. And a car waiting in the alley."

We made it along narrow corridors smelling of chlorine and through a steel fire door without getting spotted. Walsh started the engine and sat there a moment looking ahead.

"You know, you probably saved more than one life out there tonight, Lew," he said.

Then he slipped the Corvair into gear and headed for Jefferson Highway.

23.

It takes a while for us to realize that our lives have no plot. At first we imagine ourselves into great struggles of darkness and light, heroes in our Levi's or pajamas, impervious to the gravity that pulls down all others. Later on we contrive scenes in which the world's events circle like moons about us—like moths about our porch lights. Then at last, painfully, we begin to understand that the world doesn't even acknowledge our existence. We are the things that happen to us, the people we've known, nothing more.

Once reporters had dispersed, the mayor's office lost interest in me. Walsh helped convince police and media to conceal my name and identify me only as an employee of SeCure Corps. From Corene Davis, a citizen whose own privacy was fatally compromised and who must therefore have come to cherish that of others, I received three days later a handwritten note of thanks.

SeCure wasn't so easy.

A telegram waited for me, lodged between front door and frame. Please contact us ASAP, it said. When I went in, I found an envelope pushed under the door. Engraved letterhead inside. SeCure Corps wanted me to come to work for them as a field supervisor, overseeing all part-time and contract employees. Stock options were mentioned.

Good folks, those people down at SeCure. Stuff America's made of. Excellent management, careful planning, fine strategies. Deserve their $1.5 million net.

Except that when I got to sleep, one of them came crawling in to drag me out.

Thuds at the door—like the drums the natives use before the great doors in *King Kong*. Mystery. Ritual. Wonder. Oh my.

I was dreaming of drums in Congo Square. I was a child, with no comprehension of the languages rolling about me. I pressed close to my father, afraid. So much to be afraid of. I could feel the strange words gathering like coughs in his chest. Then I was in church humming along (since I didn't know the words) "What a Friend We Have in Jesus," looking up at stained-glass panels, parable of the prodigal son. The drums went on. At last I surfaced and slouched, not towards Bethlehem, but only the door.

"You hit that door again, I'll take your arm off," I said. *Damn* it's bright out there.

She looked sharply at me, opened her hand, lowered her arm. Then on impulse held the hand out. Slim fingers, narrow wrist. I took it. The world ached anew with possibilities.

"We've been trying to contact you, Mr. Griffin."

"We?"

"SeCure Corps. I'm Bonnie Bitler, executive vice president. *Veep*, as they say, to make me feel like one of the boys."

So much for a world awaft with possibilities. Just business as usual. But she'd have a hell of a time ever passing for one of the boys.

She wore a silk skirt and matching coat, somewhere between navy and black, with a light-blue blouse, simple strand of pearls. The skirt, cut close, fell just below her knees. She was trim and tall. Only the skin at her hands tipped her age: over forty, maybe closer to fifty.

"Sounds impressive, no? But the truth of it is that my husband Ephraim started the whole thing. Kick-started it, he used to say. Before he dropped, thirty years old, face-first into a gumbo I'd made from scratch. Four hours, I'd been at it."

"I'm sorry."

"I am too. Probably the best gumbo I ever made." She smiled. "Don't think I'm harsh. It's been a long time now."

I nodded.

"All I had to do was pick up where Ephraim left off. And before long we were big enough that all these others started coming around. Looking in the windows, sniffing at the doorsill."

"Bonnie Bitler, would you like some coffee?"

"I would, Mr. Griffin. If it's not too much trouble."

"Lew."

"Lew. Yes, please. I'd like that a lot."

She followed me out to the kitchen.

"I have no idea why I'm telling you all this."

Setting a pan of water over the burner, I shrugged. "People talk to me. Always have." I dumped beans into the grinder, worked the handle.

"I was going to just come here and offer you a job. Things don't get much simpler. But I seem to have kind of jumped track."

"Kind of." I crimped a paper towel into the plastic cone, dumped in pulverized beans, poured boiling water over. Set a pan of milk on the stove. "But lots of the time things look better from side roads."

"Will you at least consider the job?"

"Let me think about it."

"But you're not really interested."

"Generally I don't do too well, working for someone else. On the other hand, at this point I have something like ten dollars to my name. Not to mention outstanding hospital bills."

"I'm sorry: I thought you realized. Those were taken care of. We have an exemplary medical plan."

And I had someone sitting across from me who used words like exemplary in conversation. That didn't happen often.

I set a cup of *au lait* on the table before her. Went back to the stove to pour my own.

"Ephraim was no great businessman," she said. "But he liked strong men, men with principles, with integrity, and he had a fine talent for finding them, often in the most unlikely places. I like to think I have something of the same talent."

"Thank you."

"No need to. But you'll call? Let me know?"

I said I would.

She laughed, richly. "Men always say that, don't they? They'll call. And then never do."

She paused at the door. "Maybe this time *I'll* call, just to talk. Do you think that would be okay? Or that possibly we might meet somewhere, have a drink or coffee?"

I thought that would be just fine. Oh yes.

When she was gone, fully awake now, I mixed a drink, pain raking fingernails down the blackboard of every breath, took it outside and sat on what remained of the big house's front steps.

In the car Walsh had said, "This guy scares me, Lewis. Not many do. I won't feel right unless you have this." He laid my .38 on the flat shelf behind the gearshift.

He scared me, too. I remembered Esmé's face, her hand clutching at mine. I remembered the shooter scrambling over a Dumpster and through the delivery door. Remembered the cab driver's baseball bat swacking into me.

Felt like the bat was still swacking into me, every breath I took.

I had a drink, had another. Ought to carve notches in the neck of the bottle.

About four P.M. I got up and took one of the capsules the doctor had prescribed. Washed it down with gin and went back to bed.

Woke up hours later with Hosie Straughter crouched over me. Wet rag on my face. Dark outside.

"You all right, Lew? You in there, buddy? I need to call an ambulance?"

"Murgh." Something like that.

"Getting pretty scary here, Lewis. You okay or not, man?"

I struggled toward the surface. Dark up there, not light. Layer of ice I couldn't break through, but a space between water and ice, air there I could breathe.

"God*damn* it, Lewis."

I pushed the wet rag off my face.

My heart pounded. Acrid taste far back in my throat. Stomach aflop. Urgent messages dove and turned like sharks in my intestines.

"Murgh," I said, hand wrapped around his throat.

"Okay, *okay.*"

I rolled away. Ears ringing. Every nerve ending felt as though sandpaper had been taken to it.

"Tea on the floor by your right hand."

I groped and found it. Drank it off in four swallows. It got refilled. It got redrunk.

"You half human now? Regained the power of speech, at least?"

I thought so. But when I opened my mouth, we found out I hadn't.

"Let's try it again, then."

Coffee this time, black and strong. I heard cars tearing past outside, ten o'clock news from the radio in the front room. New riots on college campuses in California and the Midwest. An investigation of alleged racial discrimination on military bases in Vietnam. Twelve "Freedom Riders" in Alabama had been pulled from their bus and beaten.

"Welcome back, Lewis. Had me worried."

"I feel like hammered horse shit. Like the inside of someone's shoe."

"Well, there's an empty gin bottle and an open bottle of some kind of pills here by the bed. Could have something to do with that."

"Kind of dumb, huh?"

"Kind of. May not be the dumbest thing you'll do in your life, but it's on the list."

I put an experimental leg over the edge of the bed. Then another. Hoisted myself experimentally to a sitting position. Had to remember: keep good notes. The experiment was a success. I was reinventing the world.

"I don't suppose you looked in the icebox."

"As a matter of fact I did, hoping for beer."

"Anything in there?"

"A pizza with green stuff growing on it. Lots of green stuff. Not oregano or basil, far as I could tell. And a pot of something that may once have been chili."

"Green stuff on that too?"

"No. But it's got a nice thick layer of white on top. Penicillin, possibly."

"I need food." For the love of God, Montressor.

"Thought you might."

The experimental legs managed to carry me behind him into the kitchen. I smelled it before we got there. Looking down to be sure I wasn't drooling all over my feet.

Fried chicken from Jim's. Frankie DeNoux's home away from home. Bottom part of the paper bag several shades darker from grease.

"You want plates?"

Yeah, right. And get down the crystal and china too.

24.

Next morning, I called Sam Brown from a phone booth on Claiborne by a school painted pale blue and tangerine, the kind of color scheme I always think of as island pastel, part of the city's Caribbean heritage.

I said who I was and asked if he had anything for me.

"For you? You better believe it. You're tall man in the forest right now, Lewis. Word came down. Happen to be free this afternoon about two?"

I told him I thought I could arrange it.

"You sure you don't need to check your schedule, now?"

"Well, you know how it is: business first."

"I do, I do. Shame so many people've already forgotten that."

"What's on?"

"Second."

It took me a moment. "And who's on first."

"Why *you* are, man. I just told you that."

"You know, Brown, maybe we're in the wrong line. We could work up a few more gags, get us some bowlers and checkered suits and have our own TV show."

"Or at least a guest spot now and then on some white man's."

"There is that."

"And of course we'd have to be careful what we said, or we'd wind up blackballed like Bobbye Belle, having to move overseas because we couldn't get work in clubs here."

"Never happened. I read an article about it. All just a misunderstanding."

"Yeah. Right."

"So what work *do* we have?"

"Straight escort job. In and out, an hour, hour and a half tops."

"Whose pony are we riding?"

"Elroy Weaver."

A few years back, with a couple of other guys Weaver had formed Black Adder. It was the first truly militant organization for blacks, short on rhetoric, long on action. Adder had lots of enemies both inside the establishment, where the three of them spent a lot of time, accompanied by their Harvard lawyer, in court proceedings, and alongside the establishment, where repeated threats and escalating violence issued from white individuals and groups. Adder probably had as many enemies among its own community: older blacks terrified of rocking the boat any harder, younger ones convinced all we could do was burn the whole field down and start with a new crop.

"Big pony," I said.

"Ain't it though? A *real* dark horse. Weaver's coming in for a strategy-and-position conference with an undisclosed local organization. The Black Hand, we think. Whole thing's been kept quiet, Weaver's even using an assumed name. We pick him up at Moisant, deliver him to a motel out on Airline. That's it. From that point on, the local group takes over."

"Who's picking up the tab?"

"Not a question I ask."

"Who's on this, and how many?"

"Six of us. Our best men. I'll be out there myself—though you won't see me till we shut it down. Maybe after that we can talk about your future here at SeCure."

"Where am I in the line-up?"

"Honor guard, Lewis. Man says he wants you there in the car by him."

Which is where, four hours later, I found myself.

Elroy Weaver was a small man, wiry, with still, dark eyes that stayed on whatever he directed them toward, and below those eyes, a mouth quick to smile or laugh. He'd come off the plane with only a shoulder bag, down the ramp directly to me.

"Glad you made it, Lewis." He held out his hand.

Not much talk in the car. He asked me a few questions about myself, told me how much he missed his family, being away so much like this.

"You have family, Lewis?"

I told him about my parents and sister Francy up in Arkansas.

"See them often? Keep in touch?"

I shook my head, and he didn't pursue it.

"No family of your own, then."

No. Though not long after this, much to my surprise, there would be.

Just past Williams Boulevard a station wagon had tried to beat an oncoming van and got caught halfway through its turn, racking up a couple of other vehicles as it slewed across two lanes and into the cross street. We pulled up and took our place in line. Police and wreckers were clearing the road. Elroy sat watching the operation quietly.

This is what would happen: I'd go into the downtown library to look for another book by Camus and the librarian at the information desk would be named Janie. She'd be getting ready to leave for the day, for some reason I'd ask her, and before I knew it we'd be across the street drinking coffee.

When I told LaVerne that Janie and I were getting married, she just said, very quietly: Good luck, honey. I didn't see her for a long time then. Janie and I had a son. I got busy drinking and using the marriage to do things to myself that my anger and self-disgust alone couldn't accomplish. LaVerne wasn't all I didn't see back then.

Years went by and David, my son, was gone.

More years, and LaVerne was gone.

We began moving again, past a cop directing traffic, over scatters of gemlike glass.

"Maybe later, Lewis. Further along," Weaver said.

"Yeah. Maybe."

Further along we'll know all the answers, further along we'll understand why.

We eased down Airline past ramshackle bars, hole-in-the-wall eateries and blocky abandoned factories with grids of punched-out windows, to the Pelican Motor Hotel. *Refrigerated air* was painted on the office window. An overgrown drive-in movie lot sat across from the motel.

Time for the transfer, the hand-off. Always the weakest point.

As rehearsed back at SeCure, I got out of the car, leaving Weaver, another guard and the driver inside, and stood several paces away. After a moment Louis Creech stepped from the motel office to join me. He nodded curtly to me as he glanced toward the drive-in across the street. From the corner of my eye I caught a brief flash of light at the top of the screen over there. Could have been a reflection from a passing car. Gone as quickly as it came.

I had known the Sentry was on this job.

Now I knew where he was.

The game plan called for me to fall away at this point, passing Weaver on to Louis Creech. Meanwhile I'd circle around back, check the periphery.

I started around, and when everyone's attention seemed taken, sprinted down an alley behind the motel and a cut-rate furniture store, back up by the store's delivery docks, and across Airline.

Just as I hit the other side I looked back. Creech's head turned toward me. He lifted the walkie-talkie.

Beside the drive-in was what had probably been an automobile showroom, with walls intact but the windows that had spanned the whole storefront, and most of the roof, gone. I dove in there and raced through its junkyard floor: stacks of ancient tires, carcasses of small animals, fast-food containers, remains of campfires. At first I saw no way out. But an emergency exit finally gave way on the fourth kick.

I came back out into sunlight and open air and saw the screen only ten, twelve yards away.

Someone was scrambling away from its base toward the stand of trees behind.

Scrambling as once before he'd scrambled over a Dumpster and through a delivery door.

He was almost to the trees when his foot caught in something—weeds, a tangle of roots, a sinkhole—and he fell.

He got up, looked down, looked behind to see me advancing, and shot off into the trees.

Where I lost him.

I plunged on for some time—thrashing about, turning this way and that, stopping to listen—but there was little doubt my bucket had sprung a terminal leak.

At last I found my way back out. Traffic on Airline was picking up fast. More cars and pickups than trucks now, as people started home from work.

Sam Brown said, "Little ways off your post aren't you, Lewis?" So much for my bright future with SeCure.

I shrugged and walked over to where my pursuee had stumbled.

No doubt about it. A professional's piece, assembled by hand or made to order. Winchester bolt action, with a Zeiss 10x scope. The rifle's original barrel appeared to have been replaced. Only the receiver was attached to the stock. The new barrel was free-floating. I'd seen snipers carry similar hot rods.

Sam Brown had followed me.

"Who is he?" I said, looking up.

"*You're* the one has trouble, Lewis."

"Sam." I stood. "Now, I can't be absolutely sure, of course, but I think we can both assume this weapon is loaded. Since it hasn't been fired yet."

I was careful to avoid touching trigger and guard, places on the stock where fingerprints might be, though I knew there wouldn't be any.

"People know your shooter was on the job, Sam. You go down under here, under his rifle, he's the one did it. No one will say different."

He started to raise the walkie-talkie and stopped himself. "You're crazy, Griffin. Crazy as everyone says you are."

I shrugged. "America. I'll yield to the majority opinion. What are you going to do?"

Moments shouldered by. Twenty or thirty cars, pickups, service vehicles.

"I authentically don't know who he is, Griffin."

"How'd he get on the SeCure roster?"

"Again: I don't know. You'd have to go higher up on the chain. But my feeling is, *he* got in touch with *us*."

"Everything okay across the street? Weaver handed on safely?"

He nodded.

"Good. I need one of your men to drop me—and this—off downtown, at the central police station. That all right with you?"

He shrugged. "Sure. Why not?" Then as I started away he said: "Lewis."

I turned back.

"This is what you were after all along, right?"

I told him it was and he said he had wondered.

Never as invisible as we think. Us or our motives.

25.

"It's a Winchester, all right. Model 70, .308 caliber, two or three years old. A real hot rod. The new barrel's a Douglas Premium, floats free for maximum accuracy. Fires a 173-grain, boat-tail bullet in a metal jacket that the ballistics boys tell me can travel at close to 2,250 feet per second."

"Not the kind of thing you pick up at your local Sears."

"Not hardly."

"And it's the gun used in the shootings?"

"Probably so. They're still playing with it. And trying to track down sources. Where the Winchester came from, the barrel, scope. But usually we don't have much luck with this kind of thing. Lot of it's strictly underground."

"What about the ammunition?"

"We know where that came from: Lake City, Missouri. There's no other source. But when we go looking it'll have passed through eighteen hands and a couple of blinds and there won't be any way in hell we can trace it."

"So what do we do?"

"Hope we get lucky. That's mostly what cops do."

"You've talked to the good folks at SeCure."

"And to at least three of their lawyers. The company has no official connection with this alleged shooter, knows nothing of his identity or whereabouts, and perhaps it would be best if we did not return for any further chats without a court order."

129

"I almost had him, Don."

"So did I."

"Oh yeah? That's not the way I remember it. But thanks, man. Talk to you soon."

I hung up the phone, went over and sat at the bar. Place called Bob's I'd never been before, a few blocks town- and lakeside of Tulane and Carrollton. Lots of Bobbie Blue Bland and Jimmy Reed on the jukebox.

The bartender stepped up and looked at me without saying anything. One of those places.

"Bourbon," I said. "Preferably from a bottle with some kind of label on it."

He grabbed one out of the well (yes, it had a label) and up-ended it over a shot glass. Put the bottle back with one hand as he set the shot glass before me with the other.

"Been a long walk," someone said from the open door behind me. "I could do with one of those myself." I knew it was open because the bar had flooded with light. And since the whole place was maybe ten feet square, I didn't have to squint too hard to see who it was once I turned around.

"Is there a bar anywhere in New Orleans you *don't* frequent?"

"Course there is. Way bars are apt to come and go, sometimes they don't stay around long enough to become in-co-operated in my i-tinery."

"Their loss, I'm sure."

I signaled the bartender for two more bourbons as Doo-Wop took the seat beside me. The bartender could barely restrain himself. The joy of it all.

Doo-Wop drank off the bourbon between breaths.

"Hoping I might run into you, Captain," Doo-Wop said.

I waited. Finally I waved another drink his way.

"Many thanks." But he hadn't touched it yet. "Papa and I had a drink together over on Oak. I don't know, could of been the Oak Leaf. Papa says there's a man out there looking for something special. *On the loop*'s the way he put it. Told me, that captain friend of yours might want to know about this. You want to know about this, Captain?"

"What's the man looking for, Doo-Wop? You know?"

"You mind if I go ahead and have a taste, Captain? Tongue's near stuck to the roof of my mouth."

I told him sure, go ahead.

He put the empty glass down. "Many thanks." Then: "Man wants a Winchester, model 70. *And spare change*, Papa says to tell you. That worth something to you, Captain?"

I slapped my last ten on the bar, then picked it up and put down a fifty instead. The fifty I always carried in my shoe, under the insole, back then—to beat vagrancy laws, for bail, whatever. What the hell, I could live a few weeks off that ten. Sure I could.

"Yeah. Papa said it would be."

Doo-Wop motioned grandiosely, and the bartender loomed up like a ghost ship at the bar's horizon.

"Double brandy. And one for my friend here—whatever he wants."

"Where is this man, Doo-Wop?"

"Papa said you'd ask that."

"Right."

"Papa says come see him."

26.

"He's one of mine, Lewis."

The Oak Leaf looks like something that dragged itself, by brute force of will, out of the thirties into present time. Cypress walls, pressed-tin ceiling, rooms so narrow that people turn sideways to pass. Makes you think how the city itself is a kind of sprawling memory. A few blocks away, the Mississippi waits to flood all this. Only the Corps of Engineers, *that* brute force of will, holds it back.

"You have to understand," the old mercenary said. "None of us ever belonged—here, or anywhere else. We're a society to ourselves."

"I know a little about that, Papa."

He picked up his beer and looked through it at the meager light pushing its way through the bar's front window.

"Probably more than you realize, Lewis."

He swirled beer around the bottom of his glass, maybe looking to see if any of the light had remained there, and finished it off. I did likewise. The barkeep brought us two more.

An Irish ballad, "Kilkelly," started up on the jukebox.

"He stopped being a soldier when he started his own war," I said.

"It's not his war, Lewis. Soldiers always fight other people's wars. That's what makes them soldiers. You should know something about that, too."

"But the people he's killing aren't soldiers, Papa. This isn't abstraction and theory, some pure idea you kick about the classroom

133

or discuss over civilized martinis, white pawns here, black there. When these pawns fall down, they don't get up for the next game. They don't ever get up.''

"Hard for an old man to change."

"Not easy at any age, Papa."

He sat looking at me, finally spoke. "You understand so much more than you have any right to, Lewis, young as you are."

"I don't think I understand much of anything."

"Then you're wrong."

He looked away again.

"Going on forty years now, I always said ideas don't matter. Democracy, socialism, communism—all the same. Like changing your shirt between dances. Who the hell can tell any difference? One half-bad guy goes out and another half-bad guy slips into his place. No one even notices. You think any of them care about human rights, social progress? I tell my men: You're soldiers. Professionals. These people contracted for your services. The money matters. That, and doing a good job, doing what you were hired to do. That's all.''

It was a Hemingway moment. I understood that he wanted me to assure him somehow that violating his code was okay. And I couldn't do that. I could only wait.

Papa put his glass on the bar. It was still half full.

"I think I've had enough beer today. Enough of a lot of things." He stood.

"You need a ride, Lewis? Van's out back."

"Think I'll stick around for a drink or two."

"Lewis?"

"Yes, Papa."

"Was I wrong, too? All these years?"

"I don't know, Papa. How can we ever know?"

He stood there a moment longer, then told me where the shooter lived.

27.

The address he'd given me led to a partially converted warehouse on Julia. A walk-through florist's-and-gardening shop occupied the ground floor. Above that was a quartet of luxury apartments. The third floor represented a kind of industrial-residential Gaza Strip.

To this day I have no idea how Papa knew. I asked him once, years later, not long before he died. He grinned and settled back, wearing the robe one of the sitters had bought for him and the booties another had knitted. The entire nursing-home staff loved Papa.

"Soldier doesn't learn how to do good recon, he and his men don't last long out there, Lewis. Something I always had a particular knack for, though. Man always likes doing a thing he's good at."

I handed him a beer then and asked why he'd done it. Why he had decided to help me, someone he scarcely knew, and betray one of his own.

"Long time back, there was a young man I purely believed in. Knew things he didn't have any right to, understood even more. Kind of man that, he sets himself to it, he might even change his little corner of the world, make it a better place.

"That was me.

"Then years go by, my life goes on, and eventually this young man shows up again. A different young man, you understand—but the same in a lot of ways. How do we ever know what's right or wrong, he tells me. And I know him better than a mother knows her child. I have to hope he'll do better than I did with what's been given him. And I see him standing there at that same crossroads."

Papa settled back against his cushions.

"I think I want to watch television now, Lewis. Will you switch it to channel eight for me? And turn up the sound?"

Gaining entry was easy. I'd dressed in tan work clothes from Sears and carried both a yellow hardhat and clipboard. People seldom pay attention to generic black men going about work *they* certainly wouldn't do. So, looking officiously at my clipboard, I walked unchallenged through the ground-level shop, mounted emergency stairs to the second floor, and there, between apartments C and D, behind a narrow yellow door, found another, unmarked flight of utilitarian steel stairs.

My feet rang as I went up them thinking of suspense movies I'd seen, climactic scenes set in towers, lighthouses, factories, submarines. That Hitchcock movie where Jimmy Stewart's afraid of heights and the mannequin (he thinks it's a person) gets thrown off the tower. One Sunday when I was twelve, when we were supposed to be in Sunday-school class, my friend Gerald and I had set a chair on a table and, pushing aside a section of ceiling, begun a twenty-minute, disappointing climb into the belfry of Zion Baptist.

The door at the top of the steel stairs had a Yale pin-tumbler lock. State of the art back then. I shimmied in the tension bar and cranked the cylinder hard right. Then I slipped the snapper in among the pins, thumbing it. One by one, pins rebounded and settled, fell into place.

The door opened.

A vast, unfinished room with late afternoon's light coming through multiple windows of poor-quality glass. Bubbled and arun with fissures, each pane distorted in its own particular fashion the world outside. Ten frames of them, sixty-four panes per frame. Six hundred and forty different worlds.

At one rear corner, away from the windows, a mattress and box springs were flanked by orange crates, six of them stacked one atop another on either side and crammed with paperback books. Beneath the window two inch-thick doors on makeshift sawhorses comprised a bare banquet table. Midway in the room, on a nine by twelve cotton rug, sat a Danish Modern chair, spindly table and floor lamp: a kind of island, or raft.

Outside the windows an expanse of rooftops littered with beer bottles and pigeon droppings, pools of black tar, necks of antiquated ventilator shafts rising from them like so many Loch Ness monsters.

Beneath the improvised table a steel box filled with ammunition. .308 caliber, 173-grain, boat-tail bullets.

Milk in the tiny refrigerator had gone sour. Leftover coffee in the carafe had been there a while. The *Times-Picayune* on the floor by the bed was last week's Wednesday edition.

So while this was headquarters, command central, home base, evidently he spent much of his time *out there*.

On recon.

Way out in the world somewhere, as Buster Robinson, Robert Johnson, or John Lee Hooker would put it.

Methodically I went through what there was to go through: a plastic suitcase tucked behind the front door, boxes of foodstuff from a shelf by the toilet mounted in the corner opposite mattress and box springs, the toilet tank itself, gym bag, bookshelves. I learned that he liked Philip Atlee, Simenon and natural history, used Ipana toothpaste, drank French Market coffee, bought his clothes at Montgomery Ward and Penney's, kept a Walther PPK under his mattress.

Nothing personal anywhere.

No bulletin board scaled with news clippings about his victims. No lists. No collage of candid snapshots. No file of letters to the editor, to old lovers, to the President. No stacks of pamphlets, propaganda, messages-in-bottles.

I could wait, of course. He might be back in ten minutes with a sack of food—or in a week.

I'd been careful not to misplace anything, not to give any cue that someone had been here.

I went back down the ringing stairs, along the second-floor hallway, through the banks of plants onto Julia, and sat in a doorway opposite. Four men who could have been the shooter walked by.

Five men.

Six.

Then I remembered what Papa had told me, that first time: You want to find him, you look *up*.

I did, and saw a figure making its way over the crest of the adjoining roof.

Talk about private entrances.

He moved easily down the slope, dropped a foot or two onto his own flat roof. When he came to the edge he turned and went backward off it, body pivoting at the waist, legs snaking in at the top of one of the open window frames.

Then he was inside.

Within minutes I was, too.

Watching his back at the huge table by the windows as I eased into the room.

"Griffin, right?" he said. "From the alley that night. And the motel out on Airline." A coffee mug came into view past his right shoulder as he set it down. "You're a persistent man."

I wasn't, not really. Closer to plain stubborn than to anything else.

"I'd feel better about this if you didn't come any closer, or move around too much. I assume you know that I'm armed."

And I knew, from the way his head tracked me, that he could see me in the window glass. I just didn't know how well.

I had the gun Walsh had returned, but I wasn't going to use it.

"I have no quarrel with you, Griffin. Don't open doors that don't need opening."

I looked to the left and started as though to rush him, then twisted and dived hard right. He saw it change but had started his own turn left and couldn't pull out of it quickly enough. His right hand with the gun was coming around just as I hooked his left arm and, using my own momentum, spun him back onto the table.

To my credit, I got the handgun away from him as it came around.

To his, he rebounded off the table with a two-handed blow to my chest that put me down like a felled tree.

I felt him pulling at the gun, trying to pry it loose. Stubborn, remember? Even if I couldn't catch my breath.

Then I realized he wasn't trying any longer.

I had to breathe. Had to get up.

When I did, and got to the window, I saw him scrambling among protrusions—an ancient chimney, a low wall of some sort, an antenna—two roofs away.

By the time I got there, he was halfway up a steel ladder bolted into the next building. This building was twice as tall. Up here that's all there was to them: height, how level the roofs were, how much was in your way. Nothing else mattered. It was a lot simpler world.

I scrambled up the ladder after him, steadily gaining, and lunged over the rim of the roof just in time to see his shoe sink into a pool of soft tar. It stuck there. He stumbled. Fell.

I was almost to him when he hooked clawlike fingers into the laces and tore them out. Leaving the shoe behind, he sprinted off again, listing to the left with each jog. Quasimodo heading for his tower.

But I was closing fast.

He hopped onto a parapet, crouched for a short jump to the next roof. The wall was ancient cement, crumbling everywhere, and some-how I knew what was about to happen.

Instinctively I leapt toward him just as the wall gave way. He tried to go ahead with the jump.

I missed.

So did he.

28.

I remember standing there for what seemed like a long time looking down, wondering what all this meant, wondering if it could possibly mean *anything*. All those people senselessly, needlessly dead. Now one more.

I thought about Esmé's face falling away from me. Wondered if all my life that's what people would be doing: falling away from me, leaving. I was closer to the truth than I could know.

Over the next years, through many more departures, through the ruins of a marriage, sitting in Joe's or Binx's, in the Spasm Jazzbar or bars down along Dryades where Buster was playing, I'd think about that a lot. For a while that's about *all* I did. Read during the day, drink and think at night. Then the nights started advancing on the days.

I'd cracked my head on the parapet when I lunged to try to catch him, and standing there looking over the edge—it couldn't have been long, though it seemed that way—I felt myself tipping forward, dizzy. I stepped back, something hit me, and suddenly I was looking at sky.

Pale blue, bright. Puffy white clouds tacking slowly through it. Birds askitter.

Then something black that started at the center, grew, flew toward me, erased it all.

LaVerne's face was above me when I awoke. No sky now, only a chipped plaster ceiling, but that same pale blue. And voices that for a terrifying moment seemed not outside but within me.

"Lew? Can you hear me? Do you remember what happened?"

Other voices behind hers, all of them crowded together and indistinguishable. The whole world, when I opened my eyes again, flat, as though all its surfaces had been skimmed away and pasted onto cardboard.

I tried to clear my throat. They'd sealed it over somehow. Plaster, cement, Superglue. Rolled the stone back in place. For the love of God, Montressor.

I tried again and managed *Gurg*.

"Gurg yourself."

I wanted to tell her that ladies shouldn't talk that way, but it was going to have to wait.

Sometime later I resurfaced. Light still in the room, but dimmer now, tentative. Things gone gray, beginning to lose edges. Morning? Early evening? I turned my head to the door just in time to meet the pain and darkness rushing toward me. Sank back into that. So much easier. A simpler world.

"Lewis. Lewis."

They were dredging the dark waters for me. I drifted up again, weightless, up toward the light.

"Lew?"

"Luffen fill mecurr."

"What, honey?"

I tried again. "Love and feel my care."

"Don't I, though." She smiled, put her hand against my cheek, leaned in to kiss me. "You're going to be okay."

"Never have been."

"Yeah, well. The truth is, you have, Lew. You just never knew it."

"Where am I?"

"Touro. You were pursuing Carl Joseph."

A few static scenes staggered back, like snapshots. That narrow steel ladder. Obstacles. Clouds and blue sky. Coming up over the rim of the roof.

Then all of it.

"The shooter."

She nodded.

"When you rushed him, he went off the roof. Your head went

into the wall. Fair contest, but the wall was harder. You have a concussion, Lew. It's serious.''

It was serious, all right.

Verne believed that I had pursued the shooter and purposely killed him. So did the newspapers. *Everyone* believed I had intentionally killed him, I discovered in days to come. Again, as with Corene Davis, though this time not so anonymously, I'd become a kind of cut-rate folk hero.

Eventually I gave up trying to set others straight, gave up telling them again and again what actually happened. And after a while I wasn't sure anymore that, at some level, I hadn't hunted him down and intentionally killed him.

''How long have you been here, Verne? How long was I out?''

''Two days.''

She held a glass for me. Tepid water, an accordion-pleated straw. I drank with difficulty. My mouth and throat were a wasteland.

''You knew him, Verne.''

After a pause: ''Yes, I did.''

''There was a red dress hanging on a hook against one wall. I've seen you wear it.''

Another pause. ''He was a friend, Lew.''

''A friend. Like I'm a friend?''

She shook her head. ''No. Not like that at all.'' She looked away, then back to me. ''I didn't know the rest. Walsh told me.''

She held up the glass again for me, I drank and drifted off again.

Rushmore faces were there from time to time when I floated back up: Hosie Straughter, the Beret Brothers, Corene Davis, Elroy Weaver, Walsh, LaVerne. I was awake and dreaming at the same time. I don't know how much of this was real, how much imagined.

Walsh told me: You did it, Lew.

The Beret Brothers: The community thanks you, man. We all do.

And LaVerne said: You're important to me, Lew, more important than you'll ever know.

That part wasn't imagined.

I'd propped pillows against the wall, had the air conditioner cranked so high I had to hold down the pages of my book. Every little while, ice settled into my glass of Scotch with a faint tinkling. Downstairs, in the darkness, roaches would be swarming over counters, turning them from white to black.

Upstairs, I was making the most of convalescence.

Every couple of days Hosie would bring over an armload of books from the library, some of them favorites of his, others chosen at random. *The Plague*, Raymond Chandler, Himes, *Don Quixote, Notes of a Native Son*, Melville and Poe, Sturgeon's *More Than Human*.

It was like being a kid again, those endless drawling summers back in Arkansas when I'd read all morning, go for a swim in midafternoon, then come back and read long into the night.

A few days before, trying to understand what it was that so disturbed me about the shootings and about Carl Joseph's death, I had written down everything I could remember about the affair. It's been extremely helpful now, years later, writing this. The first part, anyway—since eventually, realizing I was getting nowhere, that I didn't understand, would never understand, I began playing with it, improvising, letting the piece go where it would.

Walsh had showed up at the hospital not long after I floated back up to stay.

"Looking at you now, Lewis," he said, "it's gonna be damn hard not to laugh aloud the next time I hear someone say black is beautiful. You look like baked birdshit."

"Colorful phrase."

He shrugged.

"You doing okay? Yeah, yeah: dumb question. There anything I can get you, do for you?"

"You can get me out of here."

"Lewis. Look at you. You got three needles in you, a couple of other things I don't even *know* what they are. You got so much bandage wrapped around your head, you look like the Invisible Man. You get up and try to walk, children are gonna scream, strong men faint."

"I hate hospitals."

"Everybody hates hospitals. You think you're some kind of special case? Listen: give it a couple of days. You still want to skip, I'll come get you myself. We got a deal?"

I nodded.

"You've been a good friend, Don."

"I hope to go on being."

He said the department thanked me, and filled me in on what they'd been able to piece together about Carl Joseph.

"There's not a lot. He left light footsteps—about the lightest anyone can, these days."

"Light footsteps and a few bodies."

Thirty-two years old, born in Mississippi, lived in and around New Orleans, or across the river in Algiers, since he was nineteen. Out of the country frequently in the late fifties, presumably working as a mercenary. Since then, when there was any record of employment at all, it was private security work. Hired out a couple of times as a bodyguard. His training had come courtesy of Uncle Sam, at the tail end of the Korean War. Didn't last long in the military, but long enough to qualify as an expert marksman. Drummed out soon after. It was a long list of charges, beginning with insubordination and running on to almost killing some guy in his barracks who used a word he didn't like. No evidence of involvement in any radical group, no literature of same in his apartment.

I remembered Joyce, I fear the big words that make us so unhappy, and thought how close to home some of that history was.

"So what was all this about?" I said.

"Who knows? Something in his head, maybe, sunk in so deep there that we won't ever be able to find out. Or something in the air: people everywhere climbing towers, mowing down citizens. *He* knew why he was doing it. It was obvious to him, the right thing, maybe the only thing. We probably won't ever know."

So some do almost manage invisibility—for themselves *and* their motives.

His rage, I thought. His outrage. His calm expression of it. That's what was so terrifying. And why at the same time, at some level (at more than one level, truthfully), I identified with him.

Not long after, in a book Hosie brought around, I would read Borges' story of Martin Fierro. After pursuing for years a fabulous desperado, Fierro at last brings him to ground. But suddenly he realizes that all along, all these years, it's himself he has been pursuing and, turning, taking his place beside the desperado, he fights at Cruz's side against his own men.

Three days later, when I was back home in my slave quarters, a visit from Bonnie Bitler gave me at least a few answers.

It was early evening. Traffic had relented and now was building again along Washington. Streetlights switched themselves on. The city had begun its transformation.

"Are you okay?" she said when I opened the door.

I nodded.

"You don't look very okay."

"Believe me, I've been through worse."

"May I come in?"

"Please." I backed out of the doorway. "Would you like anything? Coffee, a drink? Tea?"

"No, thank you."

She followed me into the kitchen. I chipped apart some ice cubes that had half melted together and dropped them in a glass, poured Scotch over.

"You sure?"

She nodded. I sipped.

"Lewis?"

Yes.

"I came to ask you something. The man they say shot all those people, Carl Joseph. Did you kill him? Pursue him, I mean, intending to kill him?"

No.

"Everyone says that you did."

No.

"Then what happened up there, Lewis?"

I told her.

"I see." The kitchen's harsh light sought out every line and wrinkle, the loose flesh at her neck and upper arms—as though she had aged twenty years since I last saw her. "Do you think I could sit?"

I led her to the niche beneath the stairway, with its two chairs. When we sat, our knees touched.

"Years ago, before I met Ephraim, when I was little more than a child, I fell in love with the man I worked for. I was certain that he was the wisest, strongest, kindest man I'd ever known, and when he gave signs of wanting more from me, I was happy to give it. I still don't regret it. And I've never held it against him, the way things turned out."

I waited.

"I got pregnant—almost immediately, as it turned out. I was sixteen, black, eighth-grade education. He was forty, owned his own business, had a family."

"And he was white."

She looked sharply up at me, nodded.

"We talked it over, and a week or so later, one day after work he took me to the bus station, bought a ticket for me. As I was climbing on, he put a thousand dollars in my hand. A fortune, back then. He even sent more money, the first few months, but then it stopped.

"The baby was born seven months later up in Tupelo. He weighed only four pounds and almost didn't make it. I named him after his father."

"Carl Joseph."

"Yes."

"Then you were his connection to SeCure."

She nodded. "I've tried to take care of him. He would never take money, you know. Too proud for that. Even though I had money to give. And not much else."

"How did Carl feel about his father?"

"He hated him—the idea of him, I should say. I could never make Carl understand how kind his father was. That, given the time, the place, the situation, he had done all he could. Once Carl was old enough, I told him about his father, tried to explain what had happened, why. I kept trying. Just *like* a white man, he'd say."

"And all those people are dead, Carl himself is dead, because he hated his father, or because he never knew him."

"It's not that simple." She lifted her hands briefly out of her lap, put them back. "What is? Carl was a troubled young man. Alcohol, drugs, dangerous friends. He quit all that finally, but it was all still there inside him, looking for a way out."

I put my hand over hers.

"I'm sorry, Bonnie."

She leaned her head against my shoulder a moment, the merest touch, then looked up.

"I'd better be getting along."

At the door she said: "I'd still like to feel I could call you sometime, or come by, if I needed to. Would that be all right?"

"Absolutely. I look forward to it."

Standing outside the door I watched her walk, straight and tall, along the path and out of sight around the big house. Another person leaving, falling away. Maybe this one would come back. Maybe, eventually, others would.

I made another drink and hauled it upstairs, picked up novelist Juan Goytisolo's autobiography *Realms of Strife*, which I'd begun that morning and was now almost done with.

Memory, Goytisolo writes at the end of his story, cannot arrest the flow of time. It can only re-create set scenes, encapsulate privileged moments, arrange memories and incidents in some arbitrary manner that, word by word, will form a book. The unbridgeable distance between act and language, the demands of the written text itself, inevitably and insidiously degrade faithfulness to reality into mere artistic exercise, sincerity into mere virtuosity, moral rigor into aesthetics. Endowed with later coherence, bolstered with clever continuities of plot and resonance, our reconstructions of the past will always be a kind of betrayal. Put down your pen, Goytisolo says, break off the narrative, limit the damage: for silence alone can keep intact our illusion of truth.

The light snapped on downstairs. Dozens of roaches scurrying for cover, the counter white again. "Lew?" LaVerne's footsteps on the stairs.

She had brought the Scotch bottle and a bowl of ice upstairs with her.

"Listen."

I read the concluding passage to her.

"I don't understand," she said. "What does that mean? Why is it important?"

I read it again as she poured drinks for us both.

"I'm not sure. I only know that it is."

Then I put the book aside as she came into my arms there on the bed. Body long and warm and supple. Always familiar, comfortable, always new and surprising.

"What have you been doing?"

I nodded toward the book.

"And drinking," she said.

"Two things I do best."

"I seem to recall something else you do pretty well. Or used to, anyway."

I told her about Bonnie coming by, what she had said. LaVerne was the only one I ever told any of that.

"I've missed you, Lew," she said.

"I know."

"You want your drink?"

"Maybe later."

As outside, the storm (have I mentioned the storm?) began to quieten.